STERN

Also by Bruce Jay Friedman

A Mother's Kisses

About Harry Towns

The Dick

The Lonely Guy's Book of Life

a novel by

BRUCE JAY FRIEDMAN

●

STERN

●

ARBOR HOUSE
LIBRARY OF
CONTEMPORARY
AMERICANA

ARBOR HOUSE   NEW YORK

To my darling Ginger

●

*Introduction to Stern
by Jack Richardson*

●

I can still remember my reaction to *Stern* when I first read it over twenty years ago. There was, of course, critical delight, since every page was marked by a sure stylistic touch and packed with fresh comic inventions. There was also the realization—and how rarely this occurs in a lifetime of reading—that Bruce Jay Friedman was an original, a writer whose way of seeing things was wholly his own. Of course, since the publication of *Stern* we have grown used to novels that twist events and characters into outlandish parodies of everyday life, and most, I fear, have given more real pleasure to their creators than to their readers. A few—the best of Thomas Pynchon and Stanley Elkin—have achieved an artistic balance between their authors' antic visions and the world we inhabit. But none has surpassed *Stern* in the ease with which the commonplace encounters of life are made both horrible and hilarious.

However, my main response to Friedman's first novel was simple wonder that it had taken so long before a

Jewish point of view of America had been written in the manner of *Stern*. After all, the use of comedy to deal with our country's darker moods was as old as *Huckleberry Finn* and as recent as Ralph Ellison's *The Invisible Man*. But Jewish life amid the shams and lunacies of America had been treated either in the heavy-handed, potboiler fashion or in the grim, well-wrought manner of Saul Bellow's *The Victim*. Even when, in *The Adventures of Augie March*, Bellow became a bit more rambunctious and declared that he intended to tackle his subject "free style," the novel's humor betrayed hardly any tension between his hero and the country in which he lived. "I am an American," says Augie at the beginning of his story with absolute confidence. Stern, under siege in his suburban house, set upon by voracious caterpillars as well as shades of bigotry that range from the genteel snub to the outright antisemitic remark, might have a wry comment to make about Augie's swaggering claim.

For Stern feels he has been dropped into enemy territory. Having moved from the loose cultural mix and easy anonymity of the city, he sees himself as an alien intruder in a gentile, commuters' world. For a time he believes he has established a truce between himself and his new neighborhood. However, one evening he is informed by his wife that when she took their son to play with a boy a few blocks away, the boy's father had roughly intervened. "No playing here for kikes," he had said, and in separating the children, had shoved her to the ground. She landed in a way that, since she was underwearless, allowed the man "to see her." Thus Friedman's hero suffers insult as a man and as a Jew, and he knows at once that he is doomed to avenge this double affront. With masterly procrastination, it takes him the length of the novel to effect the inevitable meeting, and until he does, the reader follows him through ulcers and a nervous breakdown in his effort to steel himself for a violent showdown.

The route that Friedman takes us on twists often through Stern's past and his constant effort to accommodate the American version of the hero with his heritage as a Jew. Not that Stern is steeped in Talmudic tradition. He confesses that though he made the proper noises when reading Hebrew as a boy, he understood not a word; and though he occasionally frequents synagogues to refuel his ethnic feeling, he is baffled by the legato groaning of the old men around him. Nevertheless, Stern is keenly aware of his Jewishness as something that must be maintained and defended, even though to do so means accepting a burden he could well do without. For in the world of Stern's liberal imagination, everyone would grasp the fact that existence is so filled with pain and pitfalls that, to survive, we must show one another only the deepest sympathy. This admirable desire for human harmony makes Stern wish for qualities in himself that he believes would better fit the standard American mold. In the Air Force, he views his nonflying status as being peculiarly Jewish and envies the fighter pilots' blond, crew cut world of action. Even his body, softening slowly about the hips, seems to him the result of his people's scholarly and sedentary past.

In short, Stern suffers as much from the nightmare of social stereotypes as does his adversary, "the kike man." Well before Philip Roth, in *Portnoy's Complaint*, turned the special predicament of the American Jew into a long psychiatric joke, Friedman had told the original story and gotten the first laugh.

And it is the laugh, of course, that is of final importance. Everything I have mentioned about Stern is the stuff of which somber novels are made. Indeed, as I indicated, at the time of *Stern's* appearance, this was the accepted way of handling so delicate a subject. By choosing to do otherwise, Friedman created a hero whom we were supposed neither to admire nor pity, for Stern, lovable as he is, embodies an absurd condition.

Perhaps that condition is not so acute today as it was twenty years ago, and perhaps in another hundred years readers will have to be directed to a footnote to decipher the meaning of "kike." Perhaps. But even if this were to be the case, it would not diminish the real relevance of *Stern.* The piano-playing real estate broker who consummates a profitable closing with snatches of Chopin; the doctor who demands that Stern muse upon soufflés so that the X-rays of his stomach will not turn out grainy; the Puerto Rican lovely who inhibits passions with her bursts of flowery rhetoric—these and all the other furies that rise from the pages of Friedman's novel pursue Stern past narrow ethnic boundaries into the open territory of Everyman. Barring the extinction of literate readers, the pursuit should last for a long time to come.

—Jack Richardson

•

Prologue

•

ONE DAY in early summer it seemed, miraculously, that Stern would not have to sell his house and move away. Some small blossoms had appeared on one of the black and mottled trees of what Stern called his Cancer Garden, and there was talk of a child in the neighborhood for his son, a lonely boy who sat each day in the center of Stern's lawn and sucked on blankets. Stern had found a swift new shortcut across the estate which cut his walking time down ten minutes to and from the train, and the giant gray dogs which whistled nightly across a fence and took his wrists in their mouths had grown bored and preferred to hang back and howl coldly at him from a distance. A saintlike man in brown bowler had come to Stern with a plan for a new furnace whose efficient ducts would eliminate the giant froglike oil burner that squatted in Stern's basement, grunting away his dollars and his hopes. On an impulse, Stern had flung deep-blue drapes upon the windows of his cold, carpetless bedroom, frustrating the squadron of voyeurs he imagined clung silently

9

outside from trees to watch him mount his wife. And Stern had begun to play "Billy One-Foot" again, a game in which he pretended his leg was a diabolical criminal. "I'll get that old Billy One-Foot this time," his son Donald would say, flinging his sucking blanket to the wind and attacking Stern's heavy leg. And Stern, whose leg for months had remained immobile, would lift and twirl it about once again, saying, "Oh no, you don't. No one can ever hope to defeat the powerful Billy One-Foot."

It was as though a great eraser had swept across Stern's mind, and he was ready to start fresh again, enjoying finally this strange house so far from the safety of his city.

After leaving the home-coming train on one of these new nights, Stern, a tall, round-shouldered man with pale, spreading hips, flew happily across the estate, the dogs howling him on, reached his house, and, kissing his fragrant, long-nosed wife deep in her neck, pulled off a panty thread that had been hanging from her shorts. He asked her if anything was new and she said she had taken their son Donald about a mile down the road to see the new boy she'd heard about. When the children ran together, the boy's father had stopped cutting his lawn, pushed her down, and picked up his child, saying, "No playing here for kikes."

"What do you mean he pushed you down?" Stern asked.

"He sort of pushed me. I can't remember. He shoved me and I fell in the gutter."

"Did he actually shove you?" asked Stern.

"I don't know. I don't remember. But he saw me."

"What do you mean he saw you?"

"I was wearing a skirt. I wasn't wearing anything underneath."

"And he saw you?"

10

"I think he probably did," Stern's wife said.

"How long were you down there?"

"Just a minute. I don't know. I don't want to talk about it any more. What difference does it make?"

"I didn't know you went around not wearing anything. You did that at college, but I thought you stopped doing that."

Stern knew who the man was without asking more about him and was not surprised at what he had said. The first Saturday after they moved in, Stern had driven around the sparsely populated neighborhood, smiling out the window at people and getting a few nods in return. He had then come to this man, who was standing in the middle of the road. The man had taken a long time getting out of the way, and when Stern had smiled at him, he had tilted his head incredulously, put his hands on his hips, and, with his shirt flopping madly in the wind, looked wetly in at Stern.

Stern had held the smile on his own face as he drove by, letting it get smaller and smaller and sitting very stiffly, as though he expected something to hit him on the back of the head. On one other occasion, Stern had driven by to check the man and had seen him standing on his lawn in a T-shirt, arms heavy and molded inside flapping sleeves, his head tilted once again. And then Stern had stopped driving past the man's house and, through everything that happened afterward, had blacked the man out of his mind. Yet he had waited nonetheless for the day his wife would say this to him.

There was half an hour of daylight remaining. Stern's son flew to the top of a living-room bookcase and said, "Get me down from this blazing fire," and Stern climbed after him, throwing imaginary pails of water on the boy, and then swept him down to administer artificial respira-

11

tion. They saw Popeye together on television, Stern's wife bringing them hamburgers while they watched the set. When he had eaten, Stern said he was going to see the man, and his wife for some reason said, "Be right back."

He did not take the car, wanting the walk so he could perhaps stop breathing hard. On the way over, he kept poking his fingers into his great belly, doing it harder and harder, making blotches in his white skin, to see if he could take body punches without losing his wind. He hit himself as hard as he could that way but decided that no matter how hard you did it to yourself, it wasn't the same as someone else. As he hit himself, a small temple of sweetness formed in his middle; he tried to press it aside, as though he could shove it along down to his legs, where it would be out of the way, but it would not move. The man's house was small and immaculately landscaped, but with a type of shrub Stern felt was much too commercial. It might have been considered beautiful at one time. A child's fire wagon stood outside. Stern walked past the house, near to the curb, and then walked on by it, stopping fifty yards or so away in a small wooded glade and ducking down to do some push-ups. He got up to nine, cheated another two, and when he arose, the sweetness was still there. He saw that he had gotten something on his hand, either manure or heavily fertilized earth. He wiped it on his olive-drab summer suit pants and kept wiping it as he walked back to the man's house again, past it, and on down the road to his own.

His wife was scrubbing some badly laid tile on the floor of the den, pretending the deep crevasses didn't exist. She was a long-nosed woman of twenty-nine with flaring buttocks and great eyes that seemed always on the edge of tears.

"Can you remember whether he actually shoved you

12

down?" he asked her. "Whether there was physical contact?"

"I don't remember. Maybe he didn't."

"Because if there was physical contact, that's one thing. If he just said something, well, a man can say something. I just wish you had something on under there. I didn't know you go around that way. Don't do it any more."

"Did you see him?" his wife asked.

"No," said Stern.

"It doesn't make any difference," she said, continuing on the tile.

Part One

It was a lovely house, seated in the middle of what once had been a pear orchard, and yet it had seemed way out on a limb, a giddy place to live, so far from the protection of Stern's city. Mr. Iavone, the real-estate agent who had taken Stern and his wife to the house, said, "If you like this one, it's going to be a matter of kesh. Tell me how much kesh you can raise and I'll see what I can do." Mr. Iavone was a grim, short-tempered man who had been showing them selections all day, and when they finally drove up to this one, Stern felt under obligation to buy some house, any house, since Mr. Iavone had spent so much time with them. Golden children began to spill out of it, and the one that caught Stern's attention was a blinking woman-child with sunny face and plump body tumbling out of tight clothes. Stern, had his life depended on it, would not have been able to tell whether she was a woman or a child. Iavone, in an aside to Stern, told him that the girl-woman was the reason the Spensers were selling the house, that she had taken to doing uncontrollable things in cars with high-school boys, bringing shame to Mr. Spenser, her father, who was in data systems.

The house had many rooms, a dizzying number to Stern, for whom the number of rooms was all-important. As a child he had graded the wealth of people by the number of rooms in which they lived. He himself had been brought up in three in the city and fancied people who lived in four were so much more splendid than himself.

But now he was considering a house with a wild and guilty number of rooms, enough to put a triumphant and emphatic end to his three-room status. Perhaps, Stern thought, one should do this more gradually. A three-room fellow should ease up to six, then eight, and, only at that point, up to the unlimited class. Perhaps when a three-roomer moved suddenly into an unlimited affair he would each day faint with delirium.

While Stern examined the house, Mr. Iavone sat at the piano and played selections from Chopin, gracefully swaying back and forth on the stool, his fingers, which had seemed to be real-estate ones, now suddenly full of stubby culture. (Later, Stern heard that Mr. Iavone always went to the piano for prospective buyers to show he did not drive a hard bargain. Actually, his favorite relaxation was boccie.)

Mr. Spenser, a man with purple lips and stiff neck, who seemed to Stern as though he belonged to a company that offered many benefits, walked around the house with Stern, clearing his throat a lot and talking about escrow. Stern listened, with a dignified look on his face, but did not really hear Mr. Spenser. Escrow was something that other people knew about, like stocks and bonds. "I don't want to hear about stocks," Stern's mother had once said. "It's not for our kind. Not with the way your father makes a living. There's blood on every dollar." Stern was sure now that if he stopped everything and took a fourteen-year course in escrow, he would still be unable to get the hang of it because it wasn't for his kind. Still, he felt very dignified walking around a house with a data systems man and talking about escrow. Mrs. Spenser invited Stern and his wife and child into the kitchen and brought out a jar of jam.

"Did you make that in this house?" Stern asked.

"Yes," said Mrs. Spenser, a skeletal woman Stern imagined had been worn down by her husband's dignified but fetishistic lovemaking requests.

"This is quite a house," said Stern.

The price was $27,000. Someone had told Stern always to bid $5,000 under the asking price, and, adding on $1,000 to be nice, he said, "How about $23,000?" Mr. Spenser muttered something about expediting the escrow and then said OK. Stern's heart sank. He had been willing to go to $25,000, and his face got numb, and then he began to tingle the way he once had after taking a one-penny sharpener from the five-and-ten and then waiting by the counter, unable to move, to get his Dutch Rubbing from the store owner. Getting the house as low as he had, he felt a great tenderness for Mr. Spenser; he wanted to throw his arms around the stiff-necked man, who probably knew nothing of Broadway plays with Cyril Ritchard, and say, "You fool. I just got two thousand dollars from you. How much could you get paid by your company, which probably gives you plenty of benefits but only meek Protestant salaries? Don't you know that just because a man says one price doesn't mean that's all he'll pay? You've got to hold on to those two thousands, because even though you're a churchgoer you've got a glandular daughter who'll always be doing things in cars and forcing you to move to other neighborhoods, pretending you're moving because of oil burners or escrow."

19

Mr. Iavone left the piano and said to Stern, "I see we have nice people on both sides. Would you like to leave some kesh now?"

"I want someone to see the house," said Stern.

"But you've already talked price," said Mr. Iavone. He grabbed his coat and slammed the top of the piano. "You bring people out, you're a gentleman with them, you spend the day," he said, "and you wind up holding the bag. You think they're nice people. . . . I closed three million dollars' worth of homes last year."

"I've always lived in apartments and I want someone I know to look it over. Then I'll buy it," said Stern, but Iavone slammed shut the front door. Mr. Spenser cleared his throat, and Stern was certain that the next day he would tell the other data systems people in his company about the tall, soft man who had come out, talked price, and then left without buying, the first time this had ever happened in the history of American house-buying.

"I think I'm just going to take it without doing any inspecting," said Stern. "Sometimes it's better that way." Mr. Spenser called back Iavone, who came in and said, "I knew there were nice people on both sides. If we can get the kesh settled, we'll be on our way." There was much handshaking all around, and Iavone played a jubilant march on the piano.

The closing was held several weeks later in the office of Mr. Spenser's attorney, a polite man whose barren office had only one small file in it. Stern felt a wave of pity for this attorney whose entire law practice could be squeezed into that little file cabinet. He wanted to say to him, "Stop being so polite. Be more aggressive and you'll have larger cabinets." Stern's own attorney was Saul Fleer, an immaculate man with clean fingers, who took out a little pad when he met Stern at the station and, writing, said, "The train was eighty-nine cents. I enter every penny right in here." Stern and Fleer had cokes, Fleer paying for his own and then writing "$.05" on the pad.

At the closing, Mr. Spenser and his wife sat upright, close together, their arms locked as though they were about to defend a frontier home together. Their marriage was a serious one; this was a serious, adult matter; and at such times they locked arms, sat upright, and faced things together. They blended in with their polite lawyer, and Stern had the feeling they paid him in jellies.

Stern thought Fleer drove too hard a bargain and cringed down in his seat each time Fleer, pointing a clean finger at legal papers, shouted at the Spensers' attorney, "You can get away with this out here. If I had you back in the city, you wouldn't try anything like this." Stern wanted to tell Fleer not to yell at the man, that he had only a small file.

On the matter of who should pay a certain fifty dollars, Fleer said, "I'd like to see you try a trick like this in the city."

Iavone said, "You put a gun right to my head. I have three million dollars' worth of closings a year, and this is the first time I've ever had a gun put to my head."

He walked out of the room, and, after a while, the Spensers, arms still locked, rose grimly and followed him, as though their property had been erased by an Indian raid. Their attorney, smiling politely, walked out, too. Stern wanted to be with them on the side of politeness and marital arm-linking and not have an attorney who waved fingers at people and was from the city.

"Do I have the house?" he asked.

"You saw what happened," said Fleer, stuffing papers into a briefcase, his face colored with anger. "They're strong out here. I'd like to get them in the city." Then Stern, because he didn't want Iavone to fall under his yearly three million, because the polite lawyer's tiny file touched him, and because he felt vaguely un-American, whispered, "I'll pay the fifty." Fleer said, "Aagh," and threw up his hands in disgust. Stern went to the staircase and, in a cracked voice, hollered, "Mr. Iavone." The papers were signed, and immediately afterward Iavone began calling him "Stern" instead of "Mr. Stern." At the end of the closing Mr. Spenser handed over the key, and Stern, who had always lived in the city, suddenly became frightened about being away from it. He wondered with a chill whether he really did want to live "out here."

Later that afternoon, he drove to the house with his wife and child and, as if to certify his possession of it in his own nonlegal way, Stern, in suit and tie, rolled from one end of the wide lawn to the other while his wife and child shrieked with joy. The boy had large eyes and a strange, flaring nose, and his looks changed; in the bright sun he seemed pathetically ugly, but then, coming swiftly out of a sleep, or by lamplight, hearing stories, his face seemed tender and lovely. Stern, standing on the lawn now, made up a game right on the spot called "Up in the Sky" in which he took his child under the armpits and swung him first between his legs and then up in the sky as far as he would go. On the way down once, the boy said, "Throw me up high enough to see God."

"How does he know about God?" Stern asked, a little chilled because he wasn't sure yet what God things to tell the child and hadn't counted on it coming up so early.

"A little girl on Sapphire Street where we used to live," said Stern's wife.

"God can beat up a gorilla," said the little boy as Stern flung him skyward. Stern threw him up again and again, once with viciousness, as though he really did want to lose him in the sky so that he would not have to figure out what to tell him about God.

A stab got Stern in the bottom of his wide, soft back then and he dropped to his knees and said, "Everyone on the giraffe." His wife and child got on, Stern becoming excited by the heat of her crotch. He went across the lawn carrying them, but there was a strained frivolity about the game. He wanted someone to see him, and when a car drove by, he smiled thinly, as if to say, "We're home-owners. See how much fun we always have and how we fit in." But when the one car had passed, there was no one left to show off for; in the distance there was a bleak, lonely, deserted estate, where once a man named Bagby had each Sunday skidded through the snow in a horse-drawn sleigh, entertaining his grandchildren. Stern went inside his house and walked from room to room, giving each one a number and hollering it out aloud as he stood in the center of each. "I always wanted a lot of rooms," he said, clasping his long-nosed, great-eyed wife to him. "Now look how many I've got."

After moving in officially several days later, Stern hired a trio of Italian gardeners to prepare the elaborate shrubs for summer—two old, cackling, slow-moving ones and a fragrant and temperamental young man who spoke no English but had worked on the gardens of Italian nobility. The old men made straight borders along their flower beds, but the young man did his in curlicues, standing off after each twirl and making indications of roundness in the air with his hands. Their price was three dollars an hour, and as they moved along Stern began to worry that they weren't working fast enough. He saw the shrub prepara-tion costing him $800, leaving him no money for furniture. Stern wanted to tell the young man to stop doing the time-consuming curlicued borders and to do straight ones like the old men to keep the bill down. But he was afraid to say anything to a handsome young man who had worked on the grounds of Italian nobility. Stern watched the gardeners from inside the house, ducking behind a curtain so they wouldn't see him. He hoped they would hurry and perspired as the dollars ticked away in multiples of three. The old men rested on their rakes now, poking each other and cackling obscenely at the handsome young man as he made his temperamental curlicues. Then Stern lost sight of the young man and imagined that his long-nosed, great-eyed wife had inhaled his fragrance and dragged him with a sudden frenzy into the garage, her fingers digging through his black and oily young Italian hair, loving it so much more than Stern's thinning affair, which fell out now at the touch of a comb.

But the young gardener was making tiny paths in the backyard rock garden, and when he and the two cacklers were paid and had left, Stern called his family together and said, "We've got paths. I'm a guy with paths." Even though they were narrow and largely decorative, Stern insisted his wife and child walk in and out of the paths with him, the whole child and half his wife not really fitting and spilling over onto the grass.

That night, Stern gathered his wife and son to him and they sat on the front steps of the house, Stern feeling the stone cold against his wide, soft legs, bare in Bermuda shorts. They watched it get dark, felt the air get dewy and unbalancing. "This is the best time," he said, as though he had lived ten thousand nights in houses, analyzing all the various hours of the day for quality before settling upon this one as the best. The night made him feel less jittery and isolated. Whatever bad was out there would wait until the next day. He had his boy on his lap and his wife's hips against him and he was sitting on stone steps. He might have been in the city with a thousand families all around him, ten minutes from his mother's three rooms. As he sat on the stone, a fire truck screamed to a halt before his house and a man in a fireman's uniform raced across his lawn to the steps. The man was small and had low hips with powerfully thick legs. Stern, walking through meat sections at supermarkets, had always wondered who bought the pork butts and ham hocks, strange cuts of meat Stern would never consider. It seemed to Stern that this man was probably someone who ate them, and, instead of making him undernourished, their gristle and waste went to his legs and perversely made him wiry and powerful.

"We're having a firemen's ball," the man said. "Do you want to go? The twentieth of this month."

Stern smiled in what he thought was home-owning folksiness and said, "We can't make it that night. I'm sorry."

The fireman wheeled on his trunklike legs and ran apishly back to the truck.

"You were wrong," his wife said. "Everyone buys tickets. Nobody really goes. You just give them the money."

Stern, in Bermudas, ran across the lawn, shouting, "I'll take two after all," but the truck had already screamed off, and Stern heard a voice yell "Shit" into the night.

"My first thing in this town," said Stern, "and I've got an enemy." He put his great, soft body on the stoop against his wife's hips, not at all comforted by the night now, and imagined his house with all its rooms burning to the ground, his child's hair aflame, while thick-legged firemen, deliberately sluggish, turned weak water jets on the roof, far short of the mark.

The Spensers had failed to tell Stern to spray the area, and, a month after he moved in, a caterpillar army came and attacked the grounds. When Stern first saw the insects, he said, "I'm going to get them," and went out to the lawn and began to flick them off the shrubs and then step on them when they were on the ground. But there were huge wet clumps of them on everything, and he called the spray company. "It's too early to get after them," the man said. "If you get at them too early, you just waste your spray. You've got to wait till they're sitting up perky." Stern waited a day and then called again; another voice answered and told him, "It's too late. You missed the right time. They're in there solid now."

"The other man in your place said to wait," Stern said.

"I'll rap you in the teeth you get smart," the voice screamed. "I'll come right over there and get you. You want to make trouble, I'll give you trouble all right."

Stern bought some chemicals in a store and said to his wife, "I know there are billions, but I'm going to get every one of them. This is our house." He went to work on a beautiful mountain ash tree first. There was little of it showing; the tree might as well have been one large wet caterpillar. Stern sprayed at it for an hour, until his hands were broken with blisters, but only a few caterpillars fell, not really from the potency of the chemical but simply because they lost their balance and got washed off. They were hardy when they touched the ground and Stern knew they would find their way back to the tree. He stopped spraying, and in a few days the caterpillars had left and Stern and his wife were able to see that they had attacked in a funny way, eating approximately half of everything, half of each bush and half of each shrub. In front of the house stood a wild cherry tree, lovely and fruitful on one side, black, gnarled, and cancerous on the other. The plants never went back to normal, and since it was too massive a job to replace each one, Stern and his wife learned to approach them only from certain angles, ones from which they looked complete, and pretend they were whole shrubs instead of half ones. Stern was sickened by the diseased shrubs; it was not so much their appearance that troubled him but the feeling that he had betrayed a sacred trust. "The house has been standing here for thirty years with whole shrubs," he said to his wife. "We're in it a month and there are halves."

There was, too, the dog escort problem. The house was somewhat isolated from transportation conveniences, and to get to the railroad station each day (where he left for his job in the city), Stern had to cross the huge, long-deserted estate old man Bagby had once skidded across in a sleigh. It was spread out over eighty acres and took Stern twenty-three minutes each way, much too long a walk to be brisk and refreshing. The train ride then would be an hour and six minutes, which meant that Stern would be traveling roughly three hours each day. When they had first considered the house, his wife had said, "Take the ride once. It may be too long. See how you like it." But Stern had answered, "I don't want to know about it. I love the house. If I take the ride, I may not like it and we'll never live in this house. I love this house and I don't want to know about any rides."

The estate was a lonely, windless, funereal place, terribly quiet, with many odd little buildings, and for the first weeks of walking its length Stern made it his business to investigate a different one of them each morning. On one such morning, he climbed the watchtower and stood on the second floor, looking out of the cracked windows onto huge, rolling lawns and at bushes that had holes in them, seemingly torn out at random by large fists. Stern wondered how the estate was when it was

27

new, and then he walked over to the main estate building. On an impulse, he poked his elbow through a weak door panel and looked around innocently in the clear morning as though he, too, was surprised at all the commotion. Able to open the lock now, he waited till the echo had quieted and went inside the estate building, sweating hard, and then climbed the winding steps to the second floor. Doing everything in a hurry, he stood first in the elegantly constructed floor tub of the main bedroom and then went out to the circular balcony, extended his arms, and hollered, "Throw them to the lions," to imaginary throngs below. Then he decided to take something. The rooms seemed empty, except for a packet of newspapers tied with string. Stern worked a single paper loose and, tucking it under his arm, walked swiftly down the stairs. He smelled coffee burning and then ran out the door and kept running all the way to the train, running so hard he got a pain in his chest. He did not look at the dusty newspaper until he was in the coach. It was dated 1946, and its recent vintage somehow spoiled the whole estate for him; he never went into any of the buildings again. In any case, it was not the walk through the estate each morning that troubled him so much as the walk back at night.

At the farthest corner of the estate area, near the train, stood a loosely scattered group of houses in a heavily wooded thatch. They seemed at one time to be part of the estate and were still being lived in. In darkness each night, Stern had to cross this cluster of houses. There was no easily defined road in the area, and since it was not a real community, the only light was from an occasional window; Stern had to walk through using a pocket flashlight and not really sure whether he was on someone's property. On the second night of his estate-crossing, it was not quite so dark as it was to be later on, and Stern was able to see two thin, huge dogs vault a fence that encircled one of the houses and make for him with a whistling sound. They skimmed through the night and came to an abrupt halt at his feet, their gums drawn back, teeth white, both dogs reaching high above his waist. One took Stern's wrist between his teeth, and the two animals, hugging close to his side, walked with him between them, as though they were guards taking a man to prison. Stern went along with them, not crying out, not really sure he could cry out. The houses were fairly far off; it would take a loud cry to reach them, and Stern was certain only old people lived in them and wouldn't be able to make out voices in the night. He tried not to perspire, having heard you showed your fear that way, but he wasn't able to tell whether he was or not since it was chilly. They walked a quarter of a mile with him that way, hugging him tight on both sides, until the dog released his wrist, which was soaking wet; then both turned and went back, trotting swiftly through the night. The next day, Stern bought a penknife in the station, but when the dogs vaulted the fence that evening, he was taken aback by their speed and the whistling sound. He remembered hearing once as a child that you should never draw a blade unless you really meant to use it. Deciding the blade was probably too short, he succumbed meekly and allowed the lead dog to take his wrist again. There didn't seem to be anything he could do. He had heard too that you could break a dog's back with a swift judo chop on the spine, and he took his wrist out of the dog's mouth and tapped it lightly on its leathery back, but the dog made a sound and he put his wrist back. He thought of walking up to the house from which the dogs came, but he was certain the animals were trained to kill all people who passed through the fence and would get him in the throat before he reached the door. The houses were in a

29

vague sort of grouping, not in any definite town or area, and there didn't seem to be any way to get close enough to the dog-protected house to see its address. The following day, Stern tried to guess what the address might be and called a number on the phone. An old woman's voice, hearing his, hollered, "Crumbie, crumbie," and hung up. There didn't seem to be any special police to appeal to; nor was Stern sure an ordinance was being violated. He was afraid of the police and did not want to call them anyway. He pictured the police in the section to be large, neutral-faced men with rimless glasses who would accuse him of being a newcomer making vague troublemaking charges. They would take him into a room and hit him in his large, white, soft stomach. So each night he continued to walk slowly through the estate, waiting for the dogs, almost a little relieved when they finally whistled to his side, never really sure they wouldn't decide one night to kill him in a muffled place where there would be no one to pull them off. He saw himself fighting silently in the night with the two gray dogs, lasting eight minutes and then being found a week later with open throat by small Negro children. Certain he would be killed, if not by the dogs then because his white, soft body did not seem capable of living past fifty, he called a broker one day and doubled his insurance.

There was no one to complain to. No one who could help Stern with that kind of problem. His only neighbor at the new house was an ancient man with a thin chest who was always being placed and arranged in different positions. He would be placed in the sun and then shifted to the shade when the heat got too intense for him. Then he would be moved inside and placed before the television set, great care being taken not to jostle him. In the

30

wintertime he would be shifted to a train going to Virginia, where he owned a small farm. Stern later heard that once he touched down in the South, he would leap spryly out of his wheelchair and rarely be seen in daylight without two plump-chested young girls at his side.

One bright day, the man sat vegetablelike in a folding chair, having recently been placed there by his wife. Stern, in a shining burst of weekend hope, had run out of doors with a two-pronged shovel and was loosening the earth around one of his half shrubs, hoping that the sun's warmth would get through to it and make the cancerous side blossom and start to flourish. Across a low fence, he saw his thin-chested neighbor and told him about the dogs. "They wait for me each night," he explained. With frail wrists, the man drew from his wallet a commissioner's badge and said, "I was very powerful when I had my health. I was able to get stop signs put up. Forget the dogs. I'll take care of them. Do you want to get me around a little to the east. . . " Stern shifted his neighbor around, hardly able to suppress his joy; he was thrilled to have commissioner-type power on his side and wanted to hug his neighbor's thin chest with delight. Actually he was a little afraid of him now, convinced that as a onetime commissioner he had weapons nearby and probably knew judo holds, ones you could deliver despite a thinness at the wrists. Stern looked forward to swift action, but the dogs continued to slip through the night to Stern's side until he decided the man had done nothing after all. To get any action out of him, Stern imagined his neighbor would have to be carried to the police station and placed before the chief.

The man's wife was of little help. A short woman who wore loose-flowing Alpine dirndls, she had a garbage problem and was always carrying a bagful out to a wire basket in front of her house to burn it. "I don't know where it all comes from," she would say to Stern as she made her endless pilgrimage to the basket. Often, on her way back for another load, she would see Stern across the fence, working silently to bring life back into his halves, and say, "I can remember when your house was really beautiful." Once she invited Stern and his wife into her own home. She took them into the kitchen and said, with arm extended, "This is my kitchen." Then she took them into the living room and said, "This is my living room," and so on through the house. She pointed to her husband, who had been placed in front of a fishbowl, and said, "This is my husband." Then she bid them goodbye, saying, "There was a time when your house was so lovely." She never asked them in again.

Since the summer had been cruel to him, Stern looked forward to cold weather, when he would at least not have to bother with neighbors and to face the half shrubs each day. In the winter your shrubs were not supposed to be beautiful, and Stern watched with delight as the grass faded and the leaves dropped and his half shrubs fell in with the bleakness as though their black cancer shapes were the fault of the cold and not a caterpillar miscalculation. The snow came on fast that first winter. One night it built up to eight-inch drifts and was still dropping heavily when Stern, in low-cut Italian rubbers, left the train. The dogs did not clear the fence, hanging back instead to make cold choking sounds at him in the night—as though aware that the snow would make them clumsy, unable to terrorize Stern. He was halfway across the estate when the snow piled up knee-deep and stung its way into his eyes. He bent his great back, lowered his head, and shuffled into the wind; when he had walked far enough to get to his house and still could see no lights, he knew that he had lost his way. A great pain pounded through his nose, and he could not feel his face or catch his breath. With no knowledge of the stars, he saw himself making an endless circle in the snow and then falling silently asleep in a drift, to die of frostbite yards from his new home. The wind and snow flew at him with bitterness and his face seemed to belong to a stranger. He was unable to go further and stopped, defeated by the wind, not after a forty-day trek from Point Barrow, but twenty minutes from his commuter train. Feeling ridiculous, he sat down in the snow, but then he quickly became frightened and shouted "Get me!" into the night. He napped that way for a moment, and when he awakened things were not too much better. He urinated in the snow, feeling giddy and dangerous in this white place more private than a thousand bathrooms. When the wind hit him in his open fly, he imagined himself freezing up swiftly, breaking off with a quick snap like winter wood, and he withdrew quickly with drops remaining. Then, pulling his collar together and making a serious face, he bent to the snow again, as though, by being very businesslike about it and pretending he knew exactly where he was going, the fates would somehow carry him to his door. Later, he came out of the estate, not opposite his house, but in a new part of town. He had to walk three steep hills to his house, but then, turning a corner, with everything wet upon him, he saw it suddenly, as though through a curtain drawn open quickly. It was bathed in frosty light and all its diseased half trees and shrubs were cloaked with mounds of jeweled snow. It was an enchanted candy house, the loveliest in all the world, and Stern, standing wide-hipped and breathless as though beneath a spell, enjoyed what was to be his finest moment of the winter.

Stern thought that in the cold weather he would turn his thoughts inside to family and home, creating a handsome interior that would make up for the cancer garden. He would then lead visitors swiftly through the mottled shrubs, entertain them in interior splendor, and rush them out under cover of darkness. The paint-store owner delivered gallons of paint one Saturday morning, and then, when Stern raised his brush to deliver the first dab, the owner hollered, "Don't paint." Stern lowered the brush and the man continued to shout: "Never paint. Lay your brushes aside and, for Christ's sake, don't paint. You paint and you're a fool. Uh-uh. No painting, don't paint, *never paint.*" And then he lowered his voice to a whisper and added, "Until you're *ready* to paint." He then imposed a long list of conditions which would have to be met before it would be all right for Stern to paint. "Scrape your walls, scrape your floors, paper your halls, drape your dainty pieces, test your tones, check your temp, dress properly. But, for Christ's sake, don't paint. That is, until you're ready to paint."

Stern and his wife set all the paint in the corner of the room and waited until the ideal day came along, but it never did, and they gradually lost interest in painting. It was decided they would get rolling by laying tile, and Stern's father sent Crib, an ageless Negro with great strength in his wrists, to help them lay it, his services a moving-in gift. Stern's father, a small, round-shouldered man who always wore slipovers, had worked most of his life in a shoulder pad concern for his brother, Uncle Henny, expecting to be made a partner or to take over when Henny, a coronary patient, passed on. When Henny did expire, however, the business went instead to a distant nephew who had always worked in civil service positions, and Stern's father had to continue in a subordinate position, his life more or less gone up in smoke. Crib, a sweeper and handyman, had supported Stern's father for head of the business, almost as though it had been an election, and now, years later, remained a faithful supporter of his.

"He a fair man," Crib once said to Stern. "And nobody cut a pad like him. No waste." And Stern's dad, in turn, spoke with admiration of Crib's great strength. "He must be about ninety, but he's some strong guy. You ought to see what he can lift."

Crib appeared early one morning, wide nose parched with cold, slapping himself as though he had come all forty miles on foot, and Stern, who had a special feeling for all Negroes, hugged him in a show of brotherhood. He raced upstairs to rouse his wife and bring her downstairs, long-nosed and cranky, so she could fix some bacon and eggs for the Negro. To make Crib feel at home, Stern howled with laughter as his father's friend made such remarks as "It too cold for ole Crib out here."

When Crib had cleaned his plate of eggs, Stern asked if he wanted some milk to wash them down and Crib, with a wink, said, "That ain't what I want." Catching on, Stern filled up a tumbler with rye and Crib drained it, smacking his lips. "*That* what I want," said Crib slyly, and Stern howled with laughter once again. "Now ole Crib fix you up," said the Negro, rising and going to the tile. He rolled his sleeves back over his great wrists, and Stern felt that even though tremendous power would not be needed to lay the tiles, it was comforting to have it on tap anyway. Crib spent the morning on his knees, measuring and arranging and muttering, "Ole Crib forgot his tile cutter." Stern silently placed a variety of sandwiches and another tumblerful of rye on a loose tile near Crib, and in the evening, when the job was finished, Stern's wife had a roast ready. Later, Crib went back to inspect his work, shaking his head and saying, "Crib wish he bring his tile cutter." Stern gave him twenty-five dollars, hugged him tightly, and saw him off, thinking for a moment how wonderful it would be if he could have Crib out there with him, using his great wrists to fight Stern's

35

enemies, police in rimless glasses and short, powerful-legged firemen. "You made too much of a fuss over him," said Stern's wife, and Stern replied, "He's a saint. We were lucky to get him." A day later, the tiles buckled, and Stern had to put books, *A Treasury of the World's Great Classics,* about the room to hold them down. When the *Treasury* was removed, great crevasses remained between the tiles and Stern's wife said, "We really needed him."

"We got him for nothing," said Stern. "It's not a bad job. Nobody gets tile exactly right."

But the crevasses made them suddenly lose interest in fixing up the house. They left the paint cans in the corner of the living room. The floors remained bare of carpeting, the windows without drapes. They took to ducking down when passing open windows in the nude, to avoid being spotted by cars. Upstairs, in Stern's bedroom, the color scheme remained Mr. Spenser's winter-green selection, and inferior artwork whipped up by the golden Spenser children still hung about the walls.

At this point, all of the sweetness seemed to drain out of Stern, a man who had once played a thousand inventive games with his son, Donald. There were no young children in the neighborhood for the boy to play with, and often, with the air clear and sun out full, the boy would sit alone on the front stoop, stroking a blanket, shaking quietly and trying to rock himself to sleep at the height of day. "Why do you need a blanket?" Stern would ask, and his son would answer, "I don't know." And Stern, in early morning, jittery and uncertain, an endless pilgrimage in front of him, would kneel at his wife's bed and say, "For Christ's sake, see that he has activities."

"What am I going to do out here?" she would answer, and at night, when Stern had gotten past the dogs, he would find his son standing in the middle of the lawn, holding his blanket as though he had been there all day, waiting for Stern to come back. So Stern, his stomach bursting with guilt, had made up games. A favorite had been "Butterfly Hand," in which Stern's quiet, fat hand would suddenly begin to flutter and wiggle. "It's turned into a butterfly," Stern would say to his son as it flew about the room. "There'll be no controlling it now." The hand would then go still and Stern would lift his son above his head, the boy's arms extended, for a bout of "Airplane," carrying him with droning sounds about the room and then bringing him in for tabletop landings in "San Diego." Top game of all was "Billy One-Foot," in which the boy would fight an all-out battle with Stern's leg, "Billy One-Foot, the toughest of all fighters."

They had endless thumb fights, too, but now Stern could no longer muster spirit to play the games. He would sit cold and heavy in an empty room, and when the boy said, "Let's play Billy One-Foot," Stern would pat him on the head and say, "Billy One-Foot is sick now." Occasionally, he would swing his boy round the room in a circle, clamping his own eyes shut in an effort to black out a vision of himself heaving the boy headfirst against a stone wall, forever ending thoughts of God and blankets and other children.

He had always found it amusing that his wife was lax about managing things. "You think you can get away with carelessness because your behind is beautiful," he would say, and clasp her surging buttocks. But a banister was loose that winter in their bare and windy house. It fell into no special category of repair—neither carpentry nor stairway work—and when his wife was slow to have it attended to, Stern took to shocking her with vivid accounts of what would happen because of her inaction: "Your son will fall, and perhaps when you see him at the bottom of the stairs with his head open, you'll realize the importance of having it fixed" or "A slight push on top and he'll be at the bottom dead." And Stern imagined such a scene, his son with cleaved skull and Stern unable to cry convincingly. Once, a childhood friend named Ruggie had gone to climb a fire escape and given Stern his dog's leash to hold. Stern purposely let go the leash, and the dachshund ran a mile before it went beneath a speeding car. Ruggie then came back carrying the dog in a dumb march, the dachshund's body staining his sleeves, to put him some place, while Stern watched, frozen to the ground. Now Stern imagined himself with his son's smashed body in his arms, going dumbly outside to put him someplace, too. He imagined a scene in which he was putting all the dead boy's toys in a box but continually finding new ones as years rolled by.

Stern's wife, too, became sullen, mostly about having no friends. For a while, a distant cousin of Stern's named Barbie visited and served as a companion to her. But she centered everything, the food in the middle of plates, flower vases in the center of tables. She even put Stern's son in the exact center of the couch as he watched television. Stern's wife finally wearied of her because of having to listen to her constant teen-age questions. Though she was far out of her twenties, she would ask Stern's wife, "Do you think it's sinful to allow petting on a first date?" and "Will I lose Phil if I don't let him go as far as he wants?" When she left, Stern's wife had no one, and when he asked her about this, she said, "I don't need anyone," and this infuriated Stern. "You've got to have friends," he screamed at her, and then he had a picture of all three of them, his wife, his son, himself, sitting on the lawn, sucking blankets, shaking and trying to rock themselves to sleep.

He had met his wife at college after being rejected by a young girl with musical voice and tangles of blond hair who acted in Arthur Wing Pinero plays, doing deep, curt-sying walk-ons that made Stern weak in his middle. He had scrupulously avoided taking the blond girl to bed, preferring to think of her as "not the kind of girl you do that with" until, disgustedly, she refused to see him, telling him, "Someday you'll understand." A week later, he met his wife, a girl with great eyes and shining black hair and no music in her voice, and, after an anecdote or two to establish his charm, he went with her to a black-ened golf course and, with clenched teeth and sourness, drove his fat hand through her summer-smelling petti-coats and, as she moaned "God no," kissed her and tried not to think of curtsies. Later that first night, he went into her a little, and they both froze and clung to each other. Stern at that time boarded off campus with a trembling old ex-bass fiddle player who sat each night wearing truss-like old-man belts and gadgets and twanged his instru-ment in the basement. The old man was not particularly nice to Stern. He feigned munificence by asking Stern to have glasses of milk but actually used him as a sourness tester. At night, while the old man sat in his bands and trusses, Stern would spirit the petticoated girl into his room, undressing her swiftly and then tasting and biting her, going at her with anger and closed eyes to drive away all traces of Victorian curtsies. She was the only daughter of a man who had missed great opportunities as a base-ball executive and now lived with silver tongue and fail-ing eyesight in an Oregon apartment. Her mother was Hungarian, had lost three children in infancy, and spent her time crocheting bitterly, dreaming of three dead sons. Lean of funds, they had sent the girl, with heavy trunk-loads of petticoats, for a single year of college and then

39

no more. She dated constantly, afternoons and evenings, an endless succession of boys. Stern asked her what she did on these dates and she said she'd kissed most and allowed some to "kiss her on top."

"You're the only one from New York I've known, and you're different," she said to him. "You care for different things. The others just care about being a good dresser."

Psychology interested her, but she mispronounced words, and it bothered Stern, a man who waded without joy through classics, that she had never tried Turgenev. She had total recall of her childhood and, her voice filled with pain, she told Stern tales that failed to move him. "I had twelve birds, and each time I got to love one, my parents would get rid of it. I'd come home and see it not there and look all over and then I'd realize that they'd given it away. They'd just give me enough time to love it, and then it would get out of the cage and make on the floor and my father would say, 'It's a filthy animal,' and give it to a girl friend." She was aware of her long-nosed beauty and would say to Stern, "You should have seen me at eight. I tapered off a little up through ten, but at eleven my face would have killed you. I don't even want to *talk* about my face at thirteen. I was really beautiful then, really something." She complained much of her childhood ordeals, telling Stern, "My mother never gave me sandwiches, even though she knew I would have loved them. She'd give me what was inside, and even the bread, but not sandwiches." Most of the time she would listen to Stern, though, sitting with great and shimmering eyes as he told of New York; and when he was finished, she would say, "You really are different. You're not interested in shoes or dancing. You're the most different person I know." Their talks were only bridges, and when it seemed to Stern they had put in enough time at it so that he could feel they legitimately interested one another, he would begin to kiss her and bite her and stroke her and undress her and examine her while she stood or sat calmly, great eyes shining, and let him explore her body. When he touched her a certain way they would fly at each other and she would do a private, nervous, whimpering thing beneath him. They clung to each other all over the campus, and sometimes she came to his room with nothing beneath her summer dress. She would wheel about him, nude and happy, while Stern feigned calmness and watched her with held breath as though it were a scholarly exercise. Then his loins would go weak and he would sail at her and bite her thighs too hard. He did crazy, tangled things to her, thinking he would break her frail body, but when he had finished she would come to him with great eyes wide, scrape his neck with her nails, and ask him to "be a man again." One night, after finding the very middle of her in a new way, he called her later, trembling, and said, "I shouldn't have done that to you. Let's not do it again." But they did it again the next night in his room and the fiddler opened the door, his elasticized old-man gadgets dangling, and caught them at it. Stern, in an action he could not explain, carried her, without a word to the old man, out the window and to the garden below, and they never did that thing again.

They parted for a year. She stayed in Oregon, and Stern, heavy with guilt as he stole a final bite, flew to New York in search of girls who knew Turgenev. A great singing freedom came over him, but the closest he came to a Turgenev lover in the following weeks was a divorcée's daughter who lived in midtown, tossed her hair, ate exquisitely, and said often, with appealing phoniness, "Perhaps I'll sleep with you. Perhaps I shan't." Mostly for Stern it was a time of long and lonely calls to Oregon while he tried to see how long he could stay away. One night her phone voice said, "The funniest thing. A Vene-

41

zuelan wants to marry me. He has two children, but he says he'll leave them. I just thought I'd tell you." Stern flew with nausea to Oregon in bad weather and saw her at the airport, her great eyes lovelier than before, the Venezuelan at her side. They did an intricate Latin dance for Stern, and she said, "Look what we do together. We're always dancing." Stern excused himself to vomit in the men's room, but when he emerged he pretended to be confident and the Latin took his leave. In a hotel room, she said, "You're losing your hair," and Stern said, "I don't understand this Venezuela bit."

"I enjoy his company very much," she said, and Stern, a vomit swiftly coming on, feigned coolness one last time and said, "I'm packing." She let him fold his T-shirts and then put her head deep into his lap and said, "I've been so lousy bad," and he knew he was bound to her for a hundred years.

Now, together with her in this house, it was as though a small, cold jail cell of steel had dropped out of the sky, encircling Stern's heavy body, surrounding his movement. He tried to free himself of it; he bought his son a trampoline. The boy saw it and said, "Daddy, put a rope in the sky so when I jump I'll be able to catch it and stay up there. Maybe God will catch me. God has the biggest muscle in the world." Weekend afternoons, Stern would watch his son jump sturdily on it, feeling this would build his body and protect him from banister falls. One day, the two of them heard a shot and a long crinkling of glass and saw a boy of about eighteen fly by in the street, as though he had been fired from a gun, and land on the concrete street, his arms stiffly at attention, a soldier still marching. Fingers had broken off him, and his face had swiftly turned black. Riding a motorcycle, the boy had jumped a traffic light on the corner next to Stern's house and collided with a speeding car, which had hit him head on. Stern took his son inside, not offering to be a witness, although he had seen the accident and knew the motorcycle boy was in the wrong. He just held his son tightly and kept him inside the rest of the winter, feeling the more the boy's bones grew sturdy on the trampoline, the greater chance he would be shot out of a cannon onto the concrete.

At the end of March that year, Stern went to cover his son at night and saw that the boy's head had swelled to twice its size. Stern kissed the dead side while his wife called a doctor, who said, "You've never called me before. I don't come in the middle of nights unless you're a regular patient." Stern said he would call the man and rehearsed the things he would say to him, that he had no right to call himself a doctor, that he was a peasant son of a bitch, that if he wasn't a doctor he would be selling diseased poultry to housewives. What kind of a man was he who could go to sleep while a child's fever rose and his face grew large and moonlike? He got on the phone and said, "I want to tell you that I know what you said to my wife. You wouldn't say it to a man." The doctor repeated what he had said, and Stern choked, "It's a shame."

They called a second man, Dr. Cavalucci, hesitant because of his home remedies. When Stern's chest had been inflamed or his wife's fingers had curled in shock, Cavalucci, the doctor, a soft, youthful man, wary of pills, had chuckled and begun, "Now I know this is going to sound funny, but you know those shopping bags you get at the supermarket? If you take one of them and breathe deeply into it for half an hour, you'll get to feeling better." His treatments always involved shopping bags or typewriter ribbons or old shoe polish cans, "the kind you open with a penny, brown, preferably." And he would always begin

43

his instructions by saying, "This is going to make you feel silly, but. . ." That night he touched the heavy side of the boy's face and said, "I don't have one for his case. I'm taking him in." In the ambulance, Stern held the child, but now he kissed the good side of the face, afraid of what was inside the bad one, and ashamed of himself for feeling that way, and finally kissing lightly the bad side, too. He said to the doctor, "Anything I've got. Anything I own. Just make him better." But he felt as though he were giving a performance and wondered how many other men had said the same thing. The hospital had long corridors and Stern had heard it was good but needed grants. Inside, a cluster of young men gathered round the child, and when Cavalucci said they were all fine specialists, Stern wondered if he should be calling in men from Europe. When Stern was a child, a cousin of his had once fallen in love with a dying girl, and Stern remembered hearing that he had done everything for her, even to the point of "bringing in men from Europe." The phrase "men from Europe" had stuck with Stern, and he wondered how you went about getting them. It seemed so hopeless, standing in the children's ward now, just to go to the phone and get some of them over, and yet he felt that if he were a real father he would stop at nothing and bring several across. The doctors talked near the child, and when Stern asked what they were doing, Cavalucci said that two of them didn't want to go in and disturb the area and one did. Stern asked which one wanted to disturb it, and Cavalucci pointed him out. He was the surgeon. When the conference broke up, Stern glared at him but was afraid that now the man would push home his view and not only disturb the area but also try risky, tradition-breaking techniques. They waited round the clock while the live part of the face took food, and then Stern

44

and his wife went home awhile and ate veal cutlets. They looked at each other after every bite, and when they had finished, Stern said. "He's lying there, his face as big as a house, and I just ate veal cutlets and kept them down." And then Stern wondered whether to call Winkel and whether Winkel still took cases and could come, because in his heart he still felt that all other doctors would be wrong except Winkel.

As a child, being sick had not been altogether a bad time for Stern. He would lie in his mother's bed and listen to radio shows all day, and then at night, when his fever rose, he would pull up the covers and wait to hear his father's whistle down the street, meaning he was back from work. A minute or so after the whistle, his small, round-shouldered father would stand at the bedroom door and say, "Jesus Christ . . . hmmph . . . oh, Jesus Christ," and shake his head sympathetically. Then, the first night of the sickness, Winkel would come, his hulking body supported by reedlike legs, and thump gravely at Stern's chest and back with thin, businesslike fingers. He liked cherry sodas, and Stern's mother would always have one ready for him after he finished up and washed his hands. She was a tall, voluptuous woman with dyed blond hair who wore bathrobes whenever Stern was sick. "Do you know what I would do for that man?" Stern's mother would say after Winkel had left. "I owe him my life. He's some guy." Stern's mother would then send Winkel a pair of tickets for the opera. When Stern got older, he would say, "But you paid him for coming," and his mother would answer, "You can't really pay a man like that, can you? You've got a lot of growing up to do." Winkel was always grave and unsmiling with Stern, and once when Stern had a stubborn pimple above his eye, Winkel

45

squeezed it with what seemed to Stern like hatred and said, "Love sweets, don't you?" Though Winkel later specialized in gynecology, he continued to treat Stern in his teens, and Stern's mother said, "I thank my lucky stars ten times a day I have a man like that. You have a man like that, you don't need anyone else." Nine out of ten of Stern's boyhood friends were planning to become doctors, and there was a time when Stern considered the idea too. His mother told Winkel and the doctor said, "Why doesn't he ever come up and talk to me? All the other boys come up and we have long talks." Stern did not like the sound of those long talks and never went up. He knew a little about chromosomes and Ehrlemeyer flasks, but he could not imagine ever filling up a long talk with Winkel. Later, when Stern went to college, he heard that Winkel had gone on to great eminence, giving talks on television. "I can still get him, though," his mother would say. "I'm the only one he'll still come to." Winkel had been married to a woman whose frugality supposedly made him insane. Driving from Newark to the opera one night, Winkel and his wife, so the story went, had gone off the road and into a tree, the windshield shattering and glass getting into Winkel's head. With half an hour remaining to curtain time, his wife left him in the car, forehead red, hands locked about the wheel in shock, and went to redeem the tickets. Weeks later, he ran amok while performing an appendectomy and cut two deep crosses in his kneecaps with a scalpel. Now he sat in a room, his practice gone, coming into the street only for occasional cherry sodas. Stern knew what his mother would say if Stern suggested that Winkel come look at his son. "Even with half a mind he knows more than anyone else. Do you know how big that man was? And I can still get him, too. He'll come to me in two seconds if I want him, no matter how crazy he is."

46

The swelling disappeared mysteriously one morning, and in a few days Stern, with a leaping heart, was able to carry his son into his car and back to the house. He kept his nose deep in his son's neck and marveled that some good had come out of the sickness. He had finally been among people in this bleak town, nurses and doctors and visitors in the halls. A day later, he spotted a blossom on the cancer side of the wild cherry tree—and there were other things, too, that happened quickly. A new stop sign on Stern's corner, one that would prevent motorcycle boys being shot out of cannons; a shortcut across the estate; a plan to kill his boiler; and a new attitude on the part of the dogs.

And then, of course, a week afterward, the man had said kike and looked between his wife's legs.

There were only three other occasions on which Stern and his wife discussed the kike man. One occurred the very next night when Stern, still in his topcoat, caught her wrists around the oven and said, "I just want to see how it happened."

"What do you mean?" she said.

"I want to get a picture in my mind of what it was all about. Get on the floor and show me exactly how you were. How your legs were when you were down there. It's important."

"I won't do that," she said, breaking through to clean the oven.

"I've got to see it," said Stern, grabbing her again. "Just for a second."

"I'm not going to do anything like that. I told you to forget it."

"I'm not fooling around," he said, and, taking her around the waist, he threw her to the kitchen floor, her jumper flying back above her knees.

"You crazy bastard," she said, flicking a strip of skin from his nose in a quick swipe and getting to her feet.

"All right, then—me," said Stern, getting on the floor. "My topcoat's your dress. Tell me when I'm right." He drew the coat slightly above his knees and said, "This way?"

"I'm not doing this," his wife said. "I don't know what you want me to do."

"Were you this way?" he asked. "Just tell me that."

"No," she said.

He drew the coat up higher. "This?"

"Uh-uh," she said.

He flung the overcoat back over his hips, his legs sprawling, and said, "This way?"

"Yes," she said.

Stern said, "Jesus," and ran upstairs to sink in agony upon the bed. But he felt excited, too.

On the weekend, several days later, as Stern unloaded cans of chow mein from the supermarket, his wife said, "He has big arms."

"Who?" Stern asked, knowing full well who she meant.

"The man," she said. "The man who said that thing."

"Oh," Stern said. "What do arms mean?"

The third and final time was when they sat one day beneath a birch tree while their son dug a hole in the dirt to China. The kike man drove by in his car and Stern's wife said, "I hate that man."

"You're silly," Stern said.

The man's house lay at a point equidistant between Stern's and the estate. Since Stern did not want to pass the man's house on foot anymore, he took to driving his car back and forth to the estate each day, leaving it at the estate edge each morning and picking it up at night. Once he was in his car at night, he had a choice of either

48

driving directly past the man's house or taking a more roundabout route that avoided the man's house altogether. Each night, as he boarded the train, he would begin a struggle within himself as to which road to take. The roundabout road presented the more attractive view and Stern told himself there was no earthly reason why he should have to pass up the nicer scenery along this road. The houses were much handsomer and made Stern feel he lived in a more expensive neighborhood. Stern would start off along the finer road, but when he had gone fifty yards, he would throw his car into reverse, back up, and go down the road that led past the man's house. It was much shorter this way, of course, and Stern told himself now that distance should be the only consideration, that if he took the roundabout road, he was only doing it to avoid having to look at the man's house and was being a coward, afraid that the man would pull him out of the car and break his stomach. On the few occasions when he did follow the roundabout road all the way home, he would walk past his wife and son and lie in bed, sinking his teeth into his top lip. On most occasions, however, he drove right past the man's house, going very slowly to show he knew no fear. His license said, "Driver must wear glasses," and Stern could not drive well without them, but when he went past the man's house he slipped them off to present a picture of strength, squinting for sight so he could stay on the road. Past the house, he would duck down and slip them on again, shoulders hunched in such a way that if the man was looking after Stern, he would not see the glasses.

One night Stern drove by and saw the man's son, who would have been his own son's friend, digging in the dirt beside the curb. From that night on, Stern drove very close to the curb, imagining that he would suddenly speed up, catch the boy on his bumpers, and then go the

49

remaining mile in seconds, disappearing undetected into his garage. And then he pictured a car fight in which the man would get Stern's boy, following him onto the lawn and pinning him against the drainpipe, while Stern, waiting upstairs, held his hands over his ears, blocking out the noise. The man would then, somehow, pick off Stern's wife in her kitchen and then drive upstairs and finish off Stern himself, cringing in his bedroom. Another night, Stern forced himself to examine the name on the man's mailbox. *De Luccio.* He looked it up in the telephone book that night and saw that there were eighteen others in the town. Even if he were to defeat the man, an army of relatives stood by to take his place. He wondered who he could pit against them and came up only with his married sister who lived in narrow circumstances above a store in San Diego. Once she had helped him in a snowball fight, and back to back they had done well together, until the action speeded up and ice balls began to get her in the breasts. "Stop it; she's a girl," Stern hollered, but a heavy ball split her brow and down she went, making a yowling, nasal sound. But she'd been game, standing firmly in the snow, puffing, blowing the hair out of her face, panting like a puppy. He imagined her now, back to back with him against the eighteen heavy-armed De Luccios, standing game as a puppy, until they all began to beat her breasts and easily knock her to the ground. Who else might have stood off the De Luccios? When alive, perhaps his Uncle Henny, the shoulder pad tycoon, a man of iron grip who'd been gassed in WW I. Once he had disarmed an aged knife wielder on a moving city bus. Uncle Henny would know how to handle the man. Stern could not see a picture of it in his mind, but he was sure that Uncle Henny would have been able to use his gassed lungs and steel grip to fend off the De Luccios.

His own father? There had been another De Luccio long years past, an orphan boy of supple athlete's body and golden hair who had kept Stern in terror for several years. The orphan would appear suddenly in an alley with a great laugh, fling Stern against a wall, lift him high, and drop him down, steal his jacket in the cold, and run away with it, come back, and punch Stern's eyes to slits. Stern never told his parents, afraid the orphan boy would come up to his three rooms, force his way in, and kill Stern's small father. One day, Stern stood talking to his father on the street when the orphan boy appeared, running a comb through his great piles of hair. "Who's that?" asked Stern's small father. "You know him, don't you?"

"Sort of," said Stern, his heart freezing.

"I think it's Rudy Vallee," said his father.

Others against the De Luccio army? How about his mother-in-law, the Hungarian woman? Stern's wife told him that once, as a little girl, she had been abused by a teacher and her Hungarian mother had gone to school and spat upon the antique teacher's face. Once, in an argument with his great-eyed wife, they both had sunk low and Stern had said, "Your mother didn't spit on the teacher. She peed on her." He saw her now against the De Luccios, slowly moving forward, peeing and spitting them backward until they turned on her and pummeled her old woman's stomach.

Stern took note of every detail of the man's house, a new one registering each night as he drove by. A television aerial. This was good. It meant the communications industry was getting through to the man, subtly driving home messages of Brotherhood. But he imagined the man watching only Westerns, contemptuously flicking off all shows that spoke of tolerance. Stern saw himself writing and producing a show about fair play, getting it

51

shown one night on every channel, and forcing the man to watch it since the networks would be bare of Westerns.

Empty beer cans in the garbage pail. Excellent. Enough of them, taken over a period of years, would bloat his belly and deprive his arms of power. Stern wondered how much beer it would take to run a man down physically. He felt good on nights when entire cases sat atop the garbage pail and depressed when only a few scattered cans appeared.

The man's car was of prewar vintage, neatly shined and proudly kept, and as Stern drove by in his more recent Studebaker he thought to himself, "Maybe it's an economic thing. He resents my having a newer car and a bigger house. I'll take him inside and show him my empty rooms and he'll see how foolish he is, and then we'll be friends." And other times, Stern was glad he had a newer car. He wanted to say to the man, "Think kike things and be stupid and you'll always have an old car. Act enlightened and have a new one." One night he saw the man's wife walk to the gutter to shake a broom—a stocky, square, and graceless woman whose hair was without color. Stern imagined the pair at night, coming together for a graceless, hulking lay, and for a second he felt tender toward the man. There had to be gentleness in him. Once he must have had to come to this hulking woman and court her with kindness and modesty, kike thoughts the furthest thing from his mind. But, on the following night, Stern took in a sight that made his throat turn over. As he drove by, the man was looming up in front of him, standing, hands in pockets, on the lawn and wearing a veteran's organization jacket. It meant he had come through the worst part of the Normandy campaign, knew how to hold his breath in foxholes for hours at a time and then sneak out to slit a throat in silence. He was skilled as a foot fighter and went always with deadly accuracy to a man's groin. Stern pictured him at veteran beer parties, drawing laughs with stories of the kike who'd moved in down the way a mile. He'd probably had one in his outfit, a thin and scholarly dark fellow who'd slowed down campaigns. No amount of brotherhood shows would ever make a dent in his veteran's jacket.

Frightened of the jacket, Stern realized that he had never really seen the man's face, that he knew only the heaviness of his arms, an inclination of the head, and a certain wetness at the mouth. A mailbox lay opposite the man's house, and one night Stern saved a letter and stopped his car on the corner near the box. His glasses off, he inflated his chest for an appearance of power, flexed his soft arms, and trotted to the mailbox, where he slipped in the letter, and then, facing the man's house now, trotted back to his car. Stern, his glasses on the seat, could see only that the man was hooked over his car engine and that, as he trotted back to the car, the man came out of his hook and inclined his head. But, trotting as he was, Stern could make out no details of the man's face and remained in ignorance of his features. Another night the man was nowhere in sight and Stern's eyes fixed on the license plates of his car, the two first letters registering "GS." For some reason, Stern, though he looked at the plates for several nights running, could not commit the numbers to memory. But he remembered the letters and made up a organization they might have stood for, Guardian Sons, a group of twenty who sat around on Monday nights and cackled over kikes. Each time Stern saw a prewar car with "GS" letters he was certain it was the man, just coming from a meeting, his glove compartment filled with leaflets. He seemed to see such cars everywhere. Driving past the man's house, he wondered whether he might be able to steal back in dead of night and destroy the car, dismantling the wiring, and then make it back to his own house undetected. Or could police always pick up evidence of footsteps and tire tracks? And was the man a light sleeper, nerves sharpened by combat, waiting coiled and ready to leap forward and slit throats with commando neatness?

On clear weekend days during that summer, Stern was able to look straight down the street as far as a mile or so and make out the man playing softball in the road with neighboring boys. On such days, Stern would go back inside his house, his day ruined. And often, inside the house, he would think about his Jewishness.

As a boy, Stern had been taken to holiday services, where he stood in ignorance among bowing, groaning men who wore brilliantly embroidered shawls. Stern would do some bows and occasionally let fly a complicated imitative groan, but when he sounded out he was certain one of the old genuine groaners had spotted him and knew he was issuing a phony. Stern thought it was marvelous that the old men knew exactly when to bow and knew the groans and chants and melodies by heart. He wondered if he would ever get to be one of their number. He went to Hebrew School, but there seemed to be no time at all devoted to the theatrical bows and groans, and even with three years of Hebrew School under his belt Stern still felt a loner among the chanting sufferers at synagogues. After a while he began to think you could never get to be one of the groaners through mere attendance at Hebrew School. You probably had to pick it all up in Europe. At the school, Stern learned to read Hebrew at a mile-a-minute clip. He was the fastest reader in the class, and when called upon he would race across the jagged words as though he were a long-distance track star. The meaning of the words was dealt with in advanced classes, and since Stern never got to them, he remained only a swift reader who might have been performing in Swahili or Urdu. He had two teachers, one a Mr. Lititsky, who concentrated on the technique of wearing yarmulkes and hit kids with books to keep order in the class. He had poor control over the classroom and would go from child to child, slamming an odd one here and there with a textbook and saying, "Now let's get some order here." By the time he had some, the half hour was up and there was time only for a fast demonstration of how to slip on a yarmulke. Outside, some of those slammed with books would say, "If he does that again, I'm going to hit Lititsky in the titskys," always sure to draw howls of laughter.

His other teacher was a black-eyed beauty from the Middle East named Miss Ostrow who told stories of Palestinian oases, referring to Palestine over and over as "the land of milk and honey," while Stern listened, unable to see why a land filled with those commodities should be so desirable. Miss Ostrow was beautiful and wore loosely cut Iraqi blouses, and Stern loved her, although he preferred to think of her as American-born and not to dwell on her earlier days in the Palestinian date groves. She cast him as the wicked Egyptian king, Ahasuerus, in a Purim play and, until the date of the play, called him "my handsome Ahasuerus." One day, after school, she caught Stern in a crowd in front of a drugstore and embarrassed him by standing on tiptoe and waving, "Ahasuerus."

All Hebrew School led up to the Bar Mitzvah and the singing of the Haftarah. Stern, who had a good voice, took to trilling occasional high notes in his practice Haftarah rendition, and the Haftarah coach would say, "No crooning." On the day of his Bar Mitzvah, Stern sang it flawlessly and his mother, afterward, said, "You had some voice. I could have fainted."

"Yes," said the Haftarah coach, "but there was too much crooning."

No great religious traditions were handed down to Stern by his small, round-shouldered father. He was self-conscious on the subject, and a favorite joke of his was to create some outrageous supposition, such as "Do you know why we're not allowed in the Chrysler Building after eleven at night?" When Stern or his mother would answer "Why?" Stern's small dad would say slyly, "Because we're Jews," mouthing the final word with great relish and pronouncing it "chooze." Stern's mother would then double up with laughter and Stern would join in, too. A bad punster whose favorite gag word was "homogenize" ("I homogenize saw you on the street last night"), Stern's small dad had great fun with such phrases as "orange Jews" and "grapefruit Jews." When Stern would say, "I heard that, Dad," his father would say, "Yeah, but I'll bet you never heard prune Jews."

Stern considered Passover the biggest holiday of the year, and on the first night of the celebration Stern and his parents traditionally attended a Seder in the back-room apartment of his Aunt Edda's hardware store, which was closed for the holiday. (After the final prayers, Aunt Edda switched on the lights of the store and each of the Seder-goers put in a large order for hardware items, which Aunt Edda furnished them at cost.) A small, dark-haired woman with tiny feet, Aunt Edda was much revered by the other members of the family, and Stern's mother often referred to her as a "saint" and then added, "Even though she's got more money than God." When Stern walked into Seders, Aunt Edda would run to him on tiny feet, clasp his arm, and say, "I want to tell you something," after which she would stare into his eyes, hold his arm for a long time, and then say, "You're some darling boy." Aside from arranging the Seder, Aunt Edda's main function was to thrust her tiny body into the center of the Seder fights that broke out annually. One of the main antagonists was Stern's Uncle Sweets, who presided over the ceremonies—a wild-haired man with giant lips who was involved in clandestine Chicago rackets and once, bound hand and foot, had to climb out of a lake in southern Illinois to save his life. Stern was proud of him and referred to him as "my bookie uncle." He took Stern and his parents to restaurants, always ordering meat pies and picking up the checks; outside a seafood villa once, a hobo had asked him for a handout and Uncle Sweets had put a penny in his palm and offered it to the man. When the hobo went to get it, Uncle Sweets had doubled up his palm and driven his fist into the man's nose, spreading the nose across the hobo's face with a sloshing sound Stern never forgot and leaving the man in the gutter. Stern's father said, "Hmm," and his mother said, "Oooh, Sweets is some bitch," with an excited look in her eyes. Uncle Sweets, wrapped sacredly in embroidered shawls, presided over the entire ceremony with thick lips and heavy lids, pounding his chest, quaffing wine, and singing long passages with the sweet full voice and passionate fervor of an old choir boy, as though this was his one night to atone for all the mysterious goings-on in Chicago. Challenging him each year and breaking in with his own set of more militant chants was Stern's Uncle Mackie, squat, powerfully built, burned black from the sun, a Phoenix rancher who flew in each year for Seders and to have mysterious medical things done to his "plumbing." An eccentric man who had once chased Pancho Villa deep into Mexico at General Pershing's side, Uncle Mackie, when asked about his health, would bare his perfect, gleaming teeth, double over his bronzed, military-trim body, and croak, "I feel pretty lousy." Early in the evening, he would take Stern

57

around the waist, pull him close, and whisper confidentially, "I just want to find out something. Do you still make peepee in your pants?" And then he would explode with laughter, until he checked himself, held his side, and said, "I've got to do something about the plumbing." He continued the peepee inquiries long into Stern's teens. When the Seder began, Uncle Sweets would take long difficult passages to himself, which gave him an opportunity to hit high notes galore, but soon Uncle Mackie, warming to the Seder, would break in with great clangor, doing a series of heroic-sounding but clashing chants that seemed to have been developed outdoors in Arizona. Before long, Uncle Sweets would stop and say to him, "What the hell do you know? You shit in your hat in Phoenix." And Uncle Mackie would fly at him, saying, "I'll kick your two-bit ass through the window." At this point, Aunt Edda would seize both their wrists, say, "I want to tell you something," pause for a long time, looking from one to the other, and then say, "You're both darling boys." The Seder would then continue uneasily, much tension in Uncle Sweets' choruses, Uncle Mackie continuing with much vigor but directing his efforts to another side of the room, as though trying to enlist a faction to his banner and start a split Seder. Stern wondered who he wanted to win in a fight, his bookie uncle or the peepee man who'd gone in after Pancho Villa. At the same point in every Seder, Stern's father would arise to do a brief prayer, reading in a barely perceptible whisper and in a strange accent Stern had never heard in Mr. Lititsky's class. He read uncertainly, flashing his teeth as though charm would compensate for a poor performance; others at the Seder would root him on, hollering out key words, while Stern stared at the floor, ashamed of his father's uncertain whispers and wishing he had a militant chanter for a dad. Toward the tail end of the Seder, Stern and his cousin

Flip would sneak off to the bedroom, get a dictionary, and look up dirty words, such as "vulva" and "pudendum." They would then open their flies and compare pubic hair growths, Flip's always being further along since he was six months the elder. They would generally emerge in time for Uncle Gunther's entrance. A onetime Hollywood bit player who had done harem scenes in silents, Gunther worked a lathe in a ball bearing factory, drank heavily, and was always striding into speeding cars. Tension generally built throughout Seders as to whether he'd make it this year; when he did show, there would be great relief that he hadn't gotten caught on a fender. Aunt Edda would fix him an abbreviated Seder meal, and when he had finished it, the others would begin to confer gifts upon him in deference to his lowly lathe job. Uncle Gunther would wave them off disdainfully, saying, "What do you think I am," and finally race out the door and into the street, with the others behind, still thrusting forth their gifts, a crumpled twenty-dollar bill from Uncle Sweets, advice on life from Uncle Mackie of the Far West. Stern's small father would always take off an item of clothing, a vest or belt, and holler, "What do I need it for, you fool," at the fleeing Gunther, who would stop after a while, collect the items, and allow himself to be ushered back to the store, defeated; there, Aunt Edda stood waiting for him, holding sets of pots and pans and the uneaten Seder food, wrapped in packages and tied with string. And thus the curtain would come down on another religious holiday.

The most religious person Stern knew was his grandmother, who opened the neighborhood synagogue each morning at five-thirty in cold weather or warm. In arguments with friends as to whose grandmother was more religious, Stern would weigh in with "Mine *opens* the damned synagogue," and he would generally walk off with the honors. A woman of indeterminate age with long silver hair kept in a bun, she lived out her last years in a small flat in a house near Stern's apartment building, which she shared with another grandmother. Since her own flat faced a back alley and had no front windows, she would come and spend most of the day in Stern's apartment, where she could sit at the window, look out, and see light and people. Most of the day she prayed, bowing and singing softly and wetting the pages of her prayer book as she slapped them along. She wore coat sweaters and had long breasts that hung down to her waist; Stern, horrified by them, wondered nevertheless what old women's breasts were like—yet hoped he'd never have to look at a set. When she was finished praying, she would look out the window and spot other grandmothers and laugh at them all for having crooked feet. Stern's father teased her, and whenever he spotted another old lady in the street, he would say, "There goes one of her buddies. Don't worry. She's got a whole mob of them organized." Her mind slipped and she buried bits of food around Stern's apartment, a piece of lettuce here, a slice of orange there, under sofa cushions and behind vases. When Stern's father found one, he would say, "She's got enough buried to feed an army. Probably got a load of money, too." Stern was going to high school during this period, and when he got home each afternoon, she would be waiting with the daily newspapers, asking Stern to explain the headlines to her since she knew little English. No matter what they said—"Strike to Tie Up Pier" or "Cold Weather to Continue"—she would take them to be an accounting of one of Hitler's misdeeds and would heap curses upon his head. Her eyesight was poor, and in the evening, when the light faded, it fell upon Stern to take her home so she would not be hit by cars in crossing the several streets on the way to the flat. Stern did not care for the job and would say, "I don't want to be walking with grandmothers." Since her wind was short, it took an agonizingly long time to get her back each night. She would grip his arm, they would walk thirty paces or so, and she would ask him to stop so she could catch her breath. During the stops, Stern would shuffle his feet and say, "Are you ready?" Sometimes, with his grandmother on his arm, he would pass friends in front of a bowling alley and he would say, "This is my grandmother," as the friends watched the pair creep by. When Stern came home from summer camp one year, he said to his mother, "Where's Granma?" And she said, "She's gone." Stern said, "What do you mean?" And his mother said, "She's not here any more. She went in my arms when you were away." People never died in Stern's family. They were either "gone" or they "went" or they "were taken." Stern said, "I see," and went inside and cried into a pillow, sorry he had laughed at her Hitler curses and wishing he could take her to her flat one more time, giving her long rests on the way. He wondered, too, whether anyone would ever "go" in his arms and, if they were an old person, what it would be like, whether their breath would be bad and whether the air would go out of their long breasts—and then he punched himself in the eyes to rid himself of such thoughts.

And so Stern loved a bowing grandmother and sat through Seder duels and could race with furious speed through books of ancient Hebrew; but there was little God to his religion. When Stern went to college in Oregon, even the trappings fell away. He told the people he met at school, "I don't care much about being a Jew. There's only one thing: each year I like to go and hear the Shofar blown on Rosh Hashanah. It sort of ties the

61

years together for me." And it was true that for a while Stern's last concession to his early Jewish days was to stand outside synagogues each year and listen to the ram's horn. It was as though listening to the ancient sound would somehow keep him just the tiniest bit Jewish, in case it turned out someday that a scorecard really was kept on people. One year he didn't go, however, and then he rarely went again, even though he kept using that "ties the years together" line when he met new girls and needed impressive attitudes. Before Stern met his wife at college and lived with the old man of dangling pelvic supports, he stayed in a boardinghouse of Jewish students, where the air was thick with self-consciousness. One of his two room-mates was a tall graceful redheaded boy with a monotonous voice that sounded as though he were in a telephone booth. His personality was limited, and since he seemed to have only one joke (When someone asked him for a match, he would answer, "Sure, my ass and your face"), he became known as "Gordon One-Gag."

"I've got lots of jokes," he would protest from inside his booth, to which Stern or the other room-mate would say, "Nonsense, One-Gag, you've only got one gag."

Stern's other room-mate was a small, flabby ex-Navy man named Footsy who had motherly-looking breasts and a large fund of anal jokes developed on shipboard. There grew up among the three a jargon and patter, all of which hinged on Jewishness. The motherly Navy man might suddenly arise during a study period, hold his stomach, and leave the room. "Where are you going?" the redhead might ask, to which Footsy would answer, "I can't stand the Jewishness in the room," bringing forth howls of amusement. Or Stern might make a remark about the weather, to which the Navy man would say, "How Jewish of you to say that." If Stern were to utter a pronouncement of any kind, one of his room-mates would invariably retort: "Said with characteristic Jewishness." Long imaginary dialogues were carried on between the redhead and the Navy man in which the redhead was a job applicant and Footsy was an employment director, reluctant to hire him. Finally, Footsy, prodded to explain why, would say briskly, "Well, if you must know, it's because of certain minority characteristics we'd rather not go into," and all in the room would break up laughing. The Navy man would often do a storm trooper imitation, in which he got to say, "Line dem opp against the fwall and commence mit the shooting," and a boy down the hall named Wiegel who had sick feet would come in and do another German officer, saying, "Brink in the Jewish child. Child, ve eff had to execute your parents." The redhead would try Mussolini in his last days, but Footsy, the Navy man, would say, "Stick to your one gag." Footsy would lie in bed for hours twisting lyrics of popular songs to get Jews into them: "Beware my foolish heart" became "Beware my Jewish heart," "Fool that I am" turned into "Jew that I am," and "I'm glad I met you, wonderful you" emerged "I'm glad you're Jewish, you wonderful Jew." Stern chipped in with a full lyric that went (to the tune of "Farmer in the Dell"):

The Jews caused the war.
The Jews caused the war.
We hate the Jews
Because they caused the war.

On occasion, the president of the boardinghouse, a short boy with quivering old-man jowls, would appear in the room and say, "These things aren't funny," after which Footsy would poke Stern in the ribs and whisper, loud enough for all to hear, "He's being *very* Jewish," and the president would stomp off, jowls in a rage.

Although much dating was done by the social club, little attention was paid to the girls of the single Jewish sorority, who wore the traditional campus skirts and sweaters but who seemed somehow an acne-ed, large-shouldered parody of the brisk, blond girls of the gentile sororities. Only sick-footed Wiegel took out what Footsy described as "laughing, dark-eyed beauties." When Wiegel announced that he'd booked another for Saturday night, Footsy would say, "But she's a pig," to which Wiegel would answer, "Yes, but you've got to date the pigs to get to the gentile queens."

Before dates, the redhead, all dressed, might stand before Stern and say, "Check my hair."

"Fine," Stern would say.

"Suit?"

"Excellent."

"Check me for Jewishness."

"Reject," Stern would say, and all would become convulsed. Footsy would then bare a womanly breast and say, "Here, One-Gag, practice on this little beauty." After dates, all would compare how they had done, in crisp, codelike sum-ups.

"Knee and conversation," the redhead might say, and Stern would add he'd gotten "elbow and upper thigh." Footsy, who took out homelier girls, would generally have come through with "outside of bra, heavy breathing, and an ear job." Then Stern and the redhead would get into their beds, turn out the lights, and listen to Footsy do a high-pitched imitation of an imaginary date being seduced by any one of the room-mates. "Oh, Gordon, you're very cute, but I can't possibly do any screwing. I'll take off my panties, but you've got to promise there'll be no screwing. You promise?" Footsy's voice was so convincing and the girl so appealing that Stern and Wiegel (who often came in late at night for the imitations, rubbing his sick feet) would beg him to do another, substituting *their* names.

Going along with the Jewish comedy routines, Stern began to call Footsy, his motherly, good-natured roommate, "Little Jew." In the morning when he woke up, he'd say, "Morning, Little Jew," and after classes he would ask, "How's Little Jew getting along?" It sounded good on Stern's tongue, nice and comfortable. He said it in two syllables, and it came out "Gee-yoo," and when he said it, he would bare his teeth and get a disgusted look on his face, which he felt would add to the irony and comic effect of the routine.

It was fun to say, and he began to call Footsy "Little Gee-yoo" at every possible opportunity, making terrible faces and then poking Footsy in the ribs with a laugh. It made him feel fine to keep saying it. One day the three room-mates were on their way to the ice-cream parlor where gentile girls hung out after class. Each time a group of girls walked by, Footsy would say to the redhead, "Tell them your one gag, One-Gag. That'll have them swarming all over us." And Stern would say to Footsy, "What did the little Gee-yoo think of that group?" At the ice-cream parlor, Stern held the door for Footsy, saying, "You first, Little Gee-yoo," and Footsy turned and said, "No more."

"What do you mean, Little Gee-yoo?"

"Don't call me that any more."

"The Little Gee-yoo doesn't like to be called Little Gee-yoo. Little Gee-yoo. Little Gee-yoo." It felt so good that Stern said it a few more times.

The three were inside the ice-cream parlor now, and Footsy said, "If you keep doing that, I have something I'll call you."

"There's nothing, Little Gee-yoo. Nothing at all."

"All right, Nose. What do you think of that? I'll call you Nose. Hello, Nose. Hello, Nose." With tweed-skirted gentile girls listening, he began to scream out the name—

"Nose, Nose. Hello, Nose. What do you say, Nose?"—until Stern, thin-faced and large-nosed at the time, flew out of the door and down the street, the cry following him back to the boardinghouse. At night the room-mates did not speak until, finally, Stern said, "OK, I won't call you the name if you don't call me 'Nose,'" to which Footsy nonchalantly said, "All right." To break the tension, the redhead said, "Let me tell you my one gag. Does anyone have a match?" And Footsy said, "Save it." There was a strain between Stern and Footsy from then on. One day Stern inadvertently called him "Little Gee-yoo" again and added, "I'm sorry. It slipped out." Instead of overlooking it graciously, Footsy said, "That's all right, Nose."

"I said I didn't mean it," Stern apologized.

"That's all right," said Footsy. "You're getting one for one."

At the end of the semester, the room-mates decided that they would separate and Stern went to live with the old man who wore elastic gadgets on his groin.

In the Air Force, Stern, recently married and swiftly packing on hip fat, felt isolated, a nonflying officer in a flying service, at a time when the jets were coming in and there was no escaping them; the air was full of strange new jet sounds and the ground reverberated with the throb of them. Somehow Stern connected his nonflying status with his Jewishness, as though flying were a golden, crew-cut, gentile thing while Jewishness was a cautious and scholarly quality that crept into engines and prevented planes from lurching off the ground with recklessness. In truth, Stern feared the sky, the myriad buttons and switches on instrument panels. He was afraid of charts with grids on them, convinced he could never master anything called grids, and he was in deadly fear of

phrases like "ultra high frequency" and "landing pattern."
He had a recurring dream in which he was a fighter pilot,
his plane attended to by a ground mechanic who re-
sented Stern's profile for spoiling the golden, blue-eyed
look of the squadron. Each day the mechanic would stand
by, neutral-faced, arms folded, while Stern, able to check
his plane only peremptorily, took off with heavy heart,
convinced wires had been crossed and would split his aircraft in mid-flight. Stern, who traveled to distant bases to
do administrative Air Force things, rode once to Califor-
nia as a guest on a general's luxury B-17, sitting alone in
the bombardier's bubble and feeling over Grand Canyon
that he had been put in a special Jewish seat and sealed
off from the camaraderie in the plane's center. After eight
hours of self-control, Stern felt the plane shudder and
then hang uncertainly for a moment as it circled a West
Coast Air Force base. He spread a thin layer of vomit
around his bubble and then kneeled inside it as the plane
landed, the pilots and other flying personnel filing by him
in silence. Cowardly Jewish vomit staining a golden aircraft.

Stern lusted after the tiny silver wings that said you
were a pilot, and once, in a Wyoming PX, he ducked his
shoulders down and slipped on a pair, crouching as he
did so that no one would see, holding his breath as though
each second might be his last. Then he took them off and
walked quickly out of the PX, feeling as though he'd
looked under a skirt. A great eagle sat atop the cap of
every Air Force officer, flying or nonflying, and there were
those in small towns, ignorant of insignia, who thought
each Air Force man was a pilot clearing the skies of Migs
above Korea. One day on Rosh Hashanah, Stern, shipped
for a two-week tour to Illinois, walked into a small-town
synagogue, his khakis starched, his brass agleam, as

though he had scored a dozen flying kills and now sought relaxation. He'd draped a tallith round his shoulders and stood, stooped with humility, in the last row of the temple, mouthing the prayer book words with all of his old speed. One by one, the congregation members, who seemed a race of Jewish midgets, turned and noticed him, and Stern, aware of their fond glances, sent forth some low groans and did several dipping knee bows he remembered from the old days. He did this to cheer them on further and to make it all the more marvelous that he, a man of the sky, took off precious flying time to pray in strange synagogues. Within minutes, the rabbi called him forward and began to heap honors upon his head. Not only was he allowed to read from the Torah but he got to kiss it, too, and then to escort it in a march around the synagogue. Ordinarily only one such honor was dealt out to a congregation member, and then only upon the occasion of a new grandson birth or wedding anniversary. The Torah back in its vault, Stern walked humbly to his seat, aware of the loving glances the tiny Jews kept shooting him. Wasn't it wonderful? A Jewish boy. A fighter. A man who had shot down planes. Yet when there's a holiday he puts on a tallith and with such sweetness comes to sit in synagogues. And did you see him pray? Even in a uniform he reads so beautifully. Stern loved it, and when they shot him glances, he responded with religious groans and dipping bows and as much humility as he could summon. When the Shofar had blown, they clustered around him, touching him, telling him what a handsome Jewish boy he was, saying how wonderful it must be to fly. They knew Jewish boys did accounting for the Army. But Stern was the first they knew who flew in planes. Dinner invitations were flung at the savior, and Stern, silent on his nonflying status, his lips sealed on the subject of his new bride, chose an orthodox watchmaker who did up timepieces for major league umpires and had a large and bovine unmarried daughter named Naomi. When Stern had finished dinner, he was left alone with the girl in a parlor that smelled of aged furniture, unchanged since it had been brought across from Albania after a pogrom. The light was subdued and Stern, belly bursting with chopped liver and noodle pudding, swiftly got her breasts out. They were large and comfortable ones, the nipples poorly placed, glancing out in opposite directions and giving her a strange, dizzying look. Stern fell upon them while the girl settled back in bovine defeat, as though she were able to tell from the sucks, greedy, anxious and lacking in tenderness, that nothing of a permanent nature would come of this, just as nothing ever came of her father's synagogue dinner invitations. She curled a finger through Stern's hair and seemed to think of the procession of dark-skinned boys who had been at her chest, wondering when a serious one would appear and want to wrap them up forever.

Stern stayed at her breasts like a thief, dizzy with adulterous glee. They were large, his wife's were small, and he stored up each minute as though it were gold. For hours he stayed upon her, expecting an exotic perfume he'd dreamed about to cascade from her bosom. The off-balance arrangement of her nipples prevented him from plunging on further; he was afraid there would be equal strangeness beneath her skirts. Then, too, the room smelled old and religious and Stern imagined himself piercing her and thereby summoning up the wrath of ancient Hebraic gods, ones who would sleep benignly as long as he stayed above the waist. She lay beneath him with cowlike patience while the night went by, and then Stern rose, said, "I have to go back now," and flew out of

69

the house, reeling with guilt, a day of flying heroism beneath his belt and four hours of capacious bosom-sucking engraved in his mind that no one could ever steal.

Stern, a non-flier in a flying service, yearned for Air Force comrades but had only friends. There were two of them, non-fliers, with parasitic functions like those of Stern. One was Neidel, the Jewish captain, a finance officer who made furtive afternoon calls to grain market brokers, picking up $20,000 in barley one day, dropping it in wheat the next. A regular officer, Neidel, pockmarked and in his forties, had never married for fear of having to divert money from soybean futures. Stern occasionally had lunch with him in Neidel's old car, telling him of gentile girls from college while Neidel sweated and wolfed down economy coleslaw sandwiches he had prepared in the bachelor officer rooms. Stern's other friend was Kekras, a Greek who had failed in jets. Once lean and blond, he drank heavily now and seemed a parody of gentile fliers, his hair grown long, his khakis soiled, his face swelled up with beer. Kekras burped a lot, said next to nothing, but was a great admirer of strength, and Stern got rises out of him only with apocryphal anecdotes of Charlie Keller, ancient Yankee outfielder. "He could carry seven baseballs in one hand," Stern would report, and Kekras would shake his head and say, "What a monster."

"Some said he could even grab eight of them in his prime."

"Jesus," Kekras would say.

"I once saw him outside of Yankee Stadium," Stern would add. "He had the bushiest eyebrows I'd ever seen on a man, and you should have seen his arms. They hung down to the ground like an ape's."

"What a horse," Kekras would say, grinning and shaking his head with affection. "What an ox." And Stern was thrilled that he was talking intimately with a gentile man of the air, even though a cast-off, heavy-lidded one whose senses were too dulled for the new jets.

Stern felt like a thief throughout his Air Force tour, a sponger and a parasite, a secret vomiter masquerading in suits of Air Force blue with great heroic eagles perched atop his garrison cap. "I'd feel more comfortable wearing a different kind of uniform than the fliers," he'd tell Kekras, while the Greek burped and wondered whether Dolph Camilli's wrists were larger round than those of Johnny Mize. Only one brief moment did Stern feel *in* the Air Force and not an unwanted guest in a hostile house, each month taking money that should have gone to fliers.

On temporary duty in Wyoming one night, Stern had taken a seat at a bar in the officers' club next to a buxom woman quickly labeled a "hooker" by the bartender— "one of the worst I've seen in this club." Stern, who felt he'd married prematurely, now prowled tormentedly after women on his tours about the globe, keeping mental track of every loveless caress, every conversation, every female contact, as though only when he'd grabbed a certain number of breasts, stroked a certain number of thighs, racked up a magic number of sleepings would he be able to relax and be married. Bracelets of lines ringed the woman's neck, and she sat enclosed in a circle of cheap perfume, but the bourbon quickly got to Stern and turned the perfume into something desirably earthy, the neck lines into lovely chevrons of sophistication. Stern imagined taking her to his staff car, stripping off her undoubtedly worn and tragic underwear, and allowing her to entertain him with slow and worldly acts of love, and then returning quickly to the bar, possibly with an easily cleared up disease upon him, but one delicious notch closer to his magic number of sleepings. Stern sidled close to the woman, an offer of a drink on his lips, when a romantic voice behind him rang out: "Come, woman, and drink my wine. I have need of company and you seem much woman to these eyes." The hooker wheeled on her seat, said, "Scuse me," to Stern, and joined the one who had called out—a husky middle-aged man with much blond hair curled romantically down over his forehead and with deep lines burned in his face. He was wearing civilian clothes and talked in a bleary-eyed, outrageously romantic way, rising gallantly for the hooker and telling her, "Woman, you're a rare one and you've wisdom in your smile." When the hooker took her seat, the romantic man shouted to Stern, "Let the Jew join us, too. I'll not close our circle to the Jew." Stern's face froze at the bar, but he came over and said, "What do you mean, Jew?" And the man slapped his shoulder and said, "Let the Jew sit and take wine with us." Stern, oddly at ease, sat down with the pair, uncomfortable only because the man was talking so loud. "Your company is good, woman," the romantic man said, leaning back and drinking deeply. "Big Jew, you warm me with your presence." He called Stern "Jew" and "Big Jew" each time he spoke to him, and he called the hooker "woman," endowing her with a universal quality, and Stern felt a nice feeling of camaraderie sitting and drinking with the pair, the romantic gentleman who might have been an aging soldier of fortune and the wise and silent hooker who had been to many places and stayed with a legion of men. He felt as though he was in a small bar in Macao, among scarred people with grave crimes in their past, at the world's end now, saying only bitter, philosophical things and waiting to die. Ava Gardner a must for the film version. The romantic man, indeed, *was* a kind of soldier of fortune, a civilian flying instructor assigned to the Air Force. He had trained a small group of Israeli pilots during the Arab-Israeli war, and he had glowing things to say of Israeli skills. "You Jews fly well, Big Jew," he said to Stern, who exulted in his words. "You fly a good plane, and my hat is off to the flying Jew. I'll drink to you, Big Jew. You do well in the sky."

"I don't actually fly myself," Stern said, but the romantic man waved him off and said, "Big Jew, you fly a deadly plane. Drink deep with me. The woman drinks well, too."

The romantic gentleman went on extolling the virtues of Jewish pilots, and each time Stern insisted that he himself was no flier, the man said, "Let the Jew be silent and drink with me as a man of the sky."

A major Stern knew from the headquarters office came over with his wife then and stood alongside the table as the gentleman cried out, "The Big Jew is a modest man. Come, Jew, and tell us of your courage."

"That's disgusting," said the major's wife, and Stern said, "He's not saying it the way you think." But then, for the sake of the new couple, he turned to the middle-aged soldier of fortune and said, "Quit that. Don't keep calling me that." The gentleman said, "I've tasted too much of wine," got to his feet unsteadily, and walked out of the club, the hooker supporting his arm. The couple sat beside Stern, but as soon as the middle-aged gentleman had gone, Stern wanted to call him back. He wanted to say to the couple, "You're wrong. He wasn't saying 'Jew' like you think. He was saying *Big Jew. Tall* Jew. He saw me as the strong and quiet Jew in a brigade of international fighters. I might have been the Big Swede or the Big Prussian, but I was the Big Jew, the quiet, silent one with bitter memories and a past of mystery, a man you could count on to slip silently through enemy lines and slit a throat, the one with skills at demolition who could blow a bridge a thousand ways, brilliant at weaponry, a quiet man with strong and magic hands who could open any safe and fix an exhausted aircraft, fly it, too, if necessary. "Send the Big Jew. He knows how to kill. He'll get through. He says little, but no one kills a man better, and it is said that when a woman has been to bed with him she will never be loved better as long as she lives."

Stern wanted to say these things to the major and his wife, just as now, ten years later, he wanted to go out of his house and say to the man who'd kiked his wife and peered between her legs, "You've got me wrong. I'm no kike. Come and see my empty house. My bank account is lean. I drive an old car, too, and Cousy thrills me at the backcourt just as you. No synagogue has seen me in ten years. It's true my hips are wide, but I have a plan for thinness. I'm no kike."

But Stern said nothing, continuing to drive hunched and tense past the man's house, until one night he saw a line of giant American flags flying thrillingly and patriotically from the man's every window. At that moment a great flower of pain billowed up within Stern's belly, filling him up gently and then settling like a parachute inside his ribs. He nursed it within him for several weeks, and then one evening, warming tea at midnight by the gas-blue light of the ancient kitchen stove, an electric shaft of pain charged through Stern's middle and flung him to the floor, his great behind slapping icily against the kitchen tile. It was as though the kike man's boot had stamped through Stern's mouth, plunging downward, elevator-swift, to lodge finally in his bowels, all the fragile and delicate things within him flung aside.

•

Part Two

•

STERN'S DOCTOR sent him first to a man with a forest of golden curls named Brewer who took pictures of his belly. Brewer had said, "Come very early; it's the only way I can get a lot of people in," and when Stern arrived, he filled him first with thick, maltlike substances, then put him inside an eyelike machine, and, taking his place on the other side of it, said, "Think of delicious dishes. Your favorites."

Stern was barefooted and wore a thin shift; the light in the streets had not yet come up and his eyes were crusted with sleep. "I may be sick," he said. "How can I think of delicious things? All right, eggs."

"Don't fool around," said the man, squinting into the machine. "I've got to get a lot of people in. Give me your favorite taste temptations; otherwise the pictures will be grainy."

"I really do like eggs," Stern said. "Late at night, when I've been out, I'd rather have them than anything."

"Are you trying to make a monkey out of me?" the man

screamed, darting away from the machine. "Do you know how many I have got to get in today? *You give me your favorites.*" He flew at Stern, fat fists clenched, blond curls shaking, like a giant, enraged baby, and Stern, frightened, said, "Soufflés, soufflés."

"That ought to do it," said the man, his eye to the machine again. "I'm not sending out any grainy pictures."

A week after the stomach pictures had been taken, Stern sat alongside an old woman with giant ankles in the outer office of Fabiola, the specialist, and it occurred to him that he would hear all the really bad news in his life in this very office; there would be today's and then, at some later date, news of lung congestions and then, finally, right here in this very room with the wallpaper and leather couches that seemed specially designed for telling people hopeless things, he would get the final word, the news that would wrap up the ball game forever. The woman beside him sorrowfully tapped her feet to an obscure Muzak ballad and, although Stern knew it was cruel, he could not help passing along his observation.

"This is a room for bad things," he said. "All the bad news in your life you get right here, right to the very end."

"I can't think now," she said, tapping away. "Not with these feet I can't."

Stern felt ashamed when he was called ahead of the giant-ankled woman, but then it occurred to him that perhaps her ankles had always been that way and were not swollen and enfeebled but sturdy with rocklike peasant power. Perhaps within her there raged fifty years more of good health; Stern was being called first because he was much further downhill, the slimness of his ankles notwithstanding.

Fabiola was a tall, brisk man who wore loose-flowing

clothes and lived in the shadow of an old doctor whose practice he had taken over, the famed Robert Lualdi, a handsome, Gable-like man who had been personal physician to Ziegfeld beauties. Somewhat senile and in retirement now, the elderly Lualdi, nevertheless, would drop in at odd times during the day, often while examinations were in session, put his feet on the young doctor's desk, and reminisce about the days when he had a practice that was "really hotcha." Once, when Fabiola was examining a young woman's chest, the old man had come into the room, pronounced her breasts "honeys," and then gone winking out the door. The interruptions kept the young doctor on edge, and he had developed a brisk style, as though trying always to wind things up and thereby head off one of the elder doctor's nostalgic visits. He was holding the pictures of Stern's stomach up to the light when Stern entered, fingers dug into his great belly, as though to prevent the parachute within from blossoming out further. "You've got one in there, all right," said Fabiola. "Beauty. You ought to see the crater. That's the price we pay for civilization."

"Got what?" Stern asked.

"An ulcer."

"Oh," said Stern. He was sorry he had let the doctor talk first; it was as though if he had burst in immediately and told Fabiola what kind of a person he was, how nice and gentle, he might have been able to convince him that he was mistaken, that Stern was simply not the kind of fellow to have an ulcer. It was as though the doctor had a valise full of them, was dealing them out to certain kinds of people, and would revoke them if presented with sound reasons for doing so. Political influence might persuade the doctor to take it back, too. Once, when Stern had been unable to get into college, his uncle had reached a Marine colonel named Treadwell, who had phoned the college and smoothed his admission. Stern felt now that if only Treadwell were to call the doctor, Fabiola would call back the ulcer and give it to someone more deserving.

"Look, I don't think I want to have one of them," Stern said, getting a little dizzy, still feeling that it was all a matter of debate and that he wasn't going to get his point across. "I'm thirty-four." When the doctor heard his age, he would see immediately that he had the wrong man and apologize for inconveniencing Stern.

"That's when they start showing up. Look, we don't have to go in there if that's what you're worried about. We get at them other ways."

"What do you mean, go in there?" said Stern. Going in there was different from simply operating. He had a vision of entire armadas of men and equipment trooping into his stomach and staying there a long time. "You mean there was even a chance you might have had to go in?"

"I don't see any reason to move in," said Fabiola. The old doctor opened the door then and, with eyes narrowed, said, "I knew I heard some tootsies in here." He limped in rakishly and took a seat next to Stern. "Excuse me," he said, "I thought you were a tootsie. My office was always full of 'em. The real cheese, too."

"I think I may be pretty sick," Stern said, and the old man rose and said, "Oh, excuse me. I'll be getting along. Well, boys, keep everything hotcha. Any tootsies, you know who to call.

"Hotcha, hotcha," he said, and winked his way out the door.

"Look," Stern said, leaning forward now. "I really don't want to have one." He felt suddenly that it was all a giant mistake, that somehow the doctor had gotten the impression he didn't *mind* having one, that it made no difference

80

to Stern one way or the other. This was his last chance to explain that he really didn't want to have one.

"I don't see what's troubling you," said Fabiola. "You'd think I'd said heart or something."

"Maybe it's the name," Stern said. "I can't even get myself to say it." It sounded to Stern like a mean little animal with a hairy face. *See the coarse-tufted, angry little ulcer, children. You must learn to avoid him because of his vicious temper. He is not nice like our friend the squirrel.* And here Stern had one running around inside him. . . .

"I can see all of this if I'd said heart," Fabiola said, beginning to write. "All right, we'll get right at her. We can do it without moving in."

"Don't write," said Stern, searching for some last-ditch argument that would force Fabiola to reconsider. The writing would make it final. If he could get Fabiola to hold off on that, perhaps a last-minute call from Colonel Treadwell would clear him.

"I wear these tight pants," Stern said. "Really tight. I think the homosexuals are influencing all the clothes we wear, and it's silly, but I wear them anyway. I can hardly breathe, I wear them so tight. Do you think that might have done it?"

"No," said Fabiola, filling up little pieces of paper with furious scribbles. "You've definitely got one in there."

Once, on a scholarship exam, Stern had gotten stuck on the very first question. There were more than four hundred to go, but, instead of hurrying on to the next, he had continued for some reason to wrestle with the first, aware that time was flying. Unable to break through on the answer, he had felt a thickness start up in his throat and then had pitched forward on the floor, later to be revived in the girls' bathroom, all chances of passing the exam up in smoke. The same thickness formed in his throat now

81

and he toppled forward into Fabiola's carpeting, not quite losing consciousness.

"I didn't say heart," Fabiola said, leaning forward. "I could understand if I'd said heart."

Helped to his feet, Stern felt better immediately. It was as though he had finally demonstrated how seriously he was opposed to having an ulcer.

"I think we ought to bed this one down for a while," the doctor said, writing again. "I know an inexpensive place. Can you get free?"

"Oh, Jesus, I've really got one then," said Stern, beginning to cry. "Can't you see that I don't want one? I'm thirty-four." Fabiola stood up and Stern looked at the doctor's softly rising paunch, encased in loose-flowing trousers, and wondered how he was able to keep it free of coarse-tufted, sharp-toothed little ulcers. Fabiola's belly had a stately, relaxed strength about it, and Stern wanted to hug it and tell the doctor about the kike man, how bad it was to drive past his house every night. Then perhaps the doctor would call the man, tell him the awful thing he'd done and that he'd better not do it any more. Or else Fabiola would ride out in a car and somehow, with the stately, dignified strength of his belly, bring the man to his knees.

"It's a little place upstate," said Fabiola, leading Stern to the door. "The way you hit the floor I think we ought to bed it down awhile. They'll be ready for you in about three days."

Stern wanted to protest. He wanted to say, "Wait a minute. You don't understand. I *really* don't want to have one. I'm not leaving this room until I don't have one any more." But the situation had become dreamlike, as though a man was coming for his throat with a razor and he was unable to cry out. "I just didn't want this," he heard himself say sweetly.

In the corridor, the old doctor winked at Stern and said, "You boys have a couple of tootsies in there?"

"I'm awfully sick," Stern said, and went out the door.

Crying in the street, Stern hailed a cab and gave the Negro driver, a scholarly-looking gentleman, his office address. "I've just been told I've got something lousy inside me," Stern said, still crying. "Jesus, how I don't want to have it in there."

"Cut him out," the man said, shaking his head emphatically, as though he were crying "Amen" at a good sermon. "He an ulcer, cut him out an' throw him 'pon the floor. He very strong, but you throw Mr. Ulcer 'pon the floor, you see how he like that. I got an uncle, he cut one out, he live to be fifty-four."

Stern wanted to tell the man that fifty-four was no target to shoot for and that there'd be no cutting, either. He wanted to say that he thought the man's advice was terrible, but he was afraid the Negro, outwardly scholarly, had once fought as a welterweight and, irked, might quickly remove his horn-rims, back Stern against a fender, and cut him to ribbons with lethal combinations. When the cab pulled up, Stern said, "I might try cutting it out," and tipped the scholarly Negro handsomely.

At a drugstore counter near his office, Stern took a seat three stools down from the owner, Doroff the druggist, a loose and boneless man whose body seemed made of liquid and who appeared to be flowing rather than leaning against the counter. He was talking to a slender girl with long, impossibly sensual legs who twisted and untwisted them as Doroff asked her where she ate certain types of food. "Where do you gopher Chinese?" Doroff asked, and when she answered, he made a negative, fishlike face and said, "Uh-uh, the only place to go in this city is a little spot named Toy's on Fifty-third. Where do you gopher French?" He kept asking her the restaurant questions, and no matter what her answer, he would shake his head in fishlike disapproval and tell her the only good place to "gopher Indian" or to "gopher Italiano." Each time he filled her in, she would spring back suddenly, as though kissed, crossing and uncrossing her legs with glee. Stern hated the fishlike Doroff for always having cute girls on stools beside him, girls who were much too appealing for the boneless druggist, and it broke Stern's heart to see this one reacting to him with such delight. He had fears that one night the two of them would "gopher Spanish" or "gopher German" together and that before she knew what happened the boneless Doroff would be floating up against her, getting to enjoy the length of her twisting legs. He wanted to say to her now, "What's so great about him knowing restaurants? Is that something to get excited about? Yours are probably as good as his. You'd never know it to look at me now, but if I weren't so upset, I could really tell you worthwhile things. I could tell you of Turgenev."

The man who had come for Stern's order was a paunchy, gray-haired counterman who had the impression that Stern was in on things, had inside information on deals and intimate goings-on. He was always asking Stern questions impossible to answer, such as "So what's going on?" and "How'd you make it today?" No matter what Stern's answer, he would wink deeply and shake with laughter. In sober moments, he would say to Stern, "I'd like to get out of here. You hear of anything doing around, let me know." He asked Stern now, "So how'd the racket go?" And when Stern said, "Usual," he let out a hysterical bellow and said, "You really got something going, don't you?" He asked Stern then, "So what'll it be?"

84

And Stern, who felt he had a thousand pounds above his belt, said, "Milk. Warm it. I've got something going on inside me." One of Fabiola's papers had said to drink milk, and Stern was anxious to get some down, picturing a warm flood of it streaming past his throat and pacifying temporarily a hairy, coarse-tufted angry little animal within him that squawked for nourishment.

"No warm," the man said. "You have to ask the boss."

Doroff had overheard the exchange. He had had fights with Stern's boss, Belavista, down the street, and now he said, "All right on the warm. Is that what you get working for Belavista? Ulcers?" Doroff's use of the plural form brought a flood of tears to Stern's eyes. Ulcers. Fabiola had spoken of only one, and now he pictured a sea of them fanning out inside him. The girl giggled and Stern knew that he had lost all chances to get at her legs. He rose, his body hooked in a curve of pain, and whispered, "I've only got one," and then flew through the drugstore muttering, "Where do you gopher this, where do you gopher that." He wanted to holler out *Where do you gopher shit?*" but he was certain Doroff would call out a number, sixty-two, and a drugstore plan would go into operation in which all eight countermen would loyally spring over the grill and trap Stern against the paperback books, hitting him in the stomach a few times and then holding him for a paid-off patrolman.

Stern, who wrote the editorial material on product labels, traveled eight floors upward to his office now, where he was greeted by his secretary, a tall, somber girl with gently rounded but sorrowful buttocks. She had lost both parents beneath a bus, and although she served Stern with loyalty, she placed a dark and downbeat cast upon all events.

85

"I've got something lousy in me and I've got to go away," Stern said. "Tell Mr. Belavista I want to see him. I've got to get wound up here so I can get out."

"What is it?" she asked. "The worst?"

"No, it's not the worst," Stern said. "But it's lousy and I'd rather not have it in there."

"Things like that take a long time to get cleared up," she said. "All right, do you want the bad news now?"

"What do you mean, bad news?" Stern asked. "All right, give it to me."

"The mail hasn't come yet and you've got someone who's been waiting on the phone."

"Is that it?" Stern asked.

"Yes," she said.

"That's not so bad," said Stern. "Why do you have to make everything sound so terrible?" She walked away and Stern studied her buttocks, rising easily beneath her black skirt. On any other girl, they would have been appealing, but he could not detach them from what he knew about her and they seemed as a consequence downbeat and sorrowful; touching them would have been reaching into a grave.

Stern picked up the phone and the voice said, "Loudon here. I've got something you're going to want and I'll only take a second."

"Something lousy happened to me," said Stern, "and I'm not doing any business. I just want to get wound up here a minute."

"I'll just be a second. Here it is. Hamburg has become the wickedest city in the world. Each year thousands of tourists troop there to visit its sin spots and to be fleeced by B-girls who know every trick of the trade. Strippers along the Reeperbahn go further than in any city in the world and, if you know the right places to go, *further*. Outwardly having no bordellos, Hamburg actually has many, and although its prosperous citizens pretend to have no knowledge of its wickedness, scratch the surface of any old-time Hamburgite and he'll direct you to the door of an establishment where flourishes the oldest profession in the world. That's about it. I go on from there detailing with anecdotes some of the more sordid practices in this bawdy city, which has replaced Paris as Europe's mecca of sin. What do you think?"

"What do you mean?" Stern asked.

"That's it. I want to do an article of say six thousand words on it for you. I can have it ready in two weeks."

"I do labels," Stern said. "For consumer products."

"You don't think you can work it in?" the voice asked.

"I do labels," Stern said. "And I don't feel good."

Stern chewed Fabiola's stomach pills and waited for his only assistant, Glover, to end his phone conversation. A tall, yellow-haired man who frowned continually, as though the sun were in his eyes, Glover spent hours on the phone each day, exchanging anecdotes with an elaborate network of friends. Glover viewed all people and listened to all remarks with pursed lips and then assigned them a rating that seemed to have been arrived at by a Board of Good Taste, staffed by witty, wafer-thin, impeccably dressed men whose job it was to continually evaluate behavior. Glover was their branch representative in Stern's office. When Stern commented on the summer heat, Glover would pause, purse his lips, and say, "You may not know it, but you've just made one of the seven best weather remarks of the season." His ratings were enervating to Stern, as when he prefaced an item of gossip by saying, "There are only five people in America who would appreciate this story. You're one of them." Stern wanted to tell him to spend less time on the phone, but he was afraid Glover, his body trim and supple from ballet exercises, would first fly at him in an effeminate rage and then pass along the episode to the Board, which would adjudge Stern "one of the three crudest men in America."

"I've got to tell you the season's funniest tapered slacks anecdote," Glover said, entering Stern's office. I'm passing this on to only four friends of mine."

"I'd like to listen, but I can't now," Stern said, certain the Board would get immediate notification of his conduct. "I've found out I've got something in me and I've got to go away for a while."

"*Growing* in you?" Glover asked, slightly amused. Stern was aware that "one of the three funniest sickness descriptions of the summer" was taking form.

"No, just in there," Stern said. "I'm not sure what it's doing." Stern had the feeling that ulcers would be frowned upon by the Board as being dirty, Jewish, unsophisticated, only for fat people, and he was careful not to identify his condition. Only dueling scars and broken legs suffered while skiing would receive high grades.

"Anyway," Stern continued, "I want you to take over and keep the labels coming." He turned his head away and said, "Long telephone calls aren't good. You might keep them short."

Glover's face swiftly filled with color. He darted toward Stern's desk with vicious ballet grace, shrieked, "*I do my work*," and Stern, frightened, whispered, "Then make long ones," and went past Glover's coiled body to Belavista's office.

Waiting outside his boss's suite, Stern felt a growing flatness and wondered suddenly whether Dr. Fabiola wasn't perhaps deceiving him and planning to "go in" after all. Stern had a memory of a glum morning long ago when he had worn a starched shirt and been brought in a taxi at dawn to have his tonsils removed. He had gone along sweetly and had not cried, feeling that something would come up, the hospital would be closed, or someone would discover his tonsils were really fine after all; but when he arrived, serious men had undressed him and brought a giant cup down over his face while he struggled and clutched at the air. Stern imagined himself sleeping at Fabiola's rest home and men stealing into his room at night with the same smothering cup.

Stern looked in now at Belavista, a middle-aged man with giant feet and large, wood-chopping teeth. He was born in Brazil, and the natural charcoal of his face was reinforced by frequent visits to Rio de Janeiro. Belavista had $3,000,000, and it was upsetting to Stern that there was no way to tell by looking at him that he had that much money. He might have been a man with $300,000 or even $27,500, and Stern felt that if you had millions, there ought to be a way for people to tell this at a glance. A badge you got to wear or a special millionaire's necktie.

Stern felt that if you had that much money, you ought to fill up every minute with $3,000,000 things, ones you couldn't do if you didn't have that much money. During conferences with Belavista, Stern found it unnerving to think that they were both spending minutes of life together in exactly the same way, despite the fact that his Latin boss had spectacular sums of money and Stern had only $800. When Belavista ordered a rare tropical fruit salad for lunch, it depressed Stern. It would come from a fine restaurant and the fruit would be of gourmet succulence, and yet it was within the reach of people who had only $300 in the bank.

Belavista was the only multimillionaire Stern had ever known, and in his presence Stern trembled with awe and barely heard his words, studying everything about him instead. He would look at his pants and think, "Oh, Jesus, inside those pants is a three-million-dollar behind, and yet the fabric can be only so soft and fine." When Belavista made a vigorous motion or even walked about the room, it would occur to Stern that he was risking a heart attack and should, if possible, always sit in chairs and not move a muscle. And yet Stern had once seen Belavista race swiftly toward a train and dive between its doors, prying them open to get aboard. Stern decided that was really the difference, that was what had made him millions. And if people had all their money and possessions taken away and everyone had to begin all over, the men who plunged daringly toward closing train doors would survive and soon have fortunes again.

Belavista was a gentle man, and Stern often told others, "He's like a father to me." Childless and divorced, Belavista lavished all his attentions on two six-year-old Brazilian nieces, listing them both as corporation directors and sending them expensive gifts. A company joke was that for a Christmas present he had once given each of them a division of IBM. Stern pictured a day in which Belavista would put his arm around him and say that his nieces were foolish, that he had always wanted a son, and would Stern consider accepting a third of the label business, leading eventually to complete control? And then Stern, all considerations of wealth aside, would have a father who leaped bravely for closing train doors.

He went in to see Belavista now and yearned for the man to put his arms around him and take him back to his many-roomed house and keep him there, protecting him from the kike man and eventually calling for his wife and boy.

"Something's come up," Stern said. "I've got to go away. They found something inside me and I have to get it taken care of."

"I'm sorry to hear that," the Brazilian said. "What is it?"

"An ulcer," Stern said. "It just showed up in there."

"Does it nag at you around here?" Belavista asked, pointing between his ribs.

"Yes," Stern said. "That's where it gets you."

"Uh-huh," said Belavista. "I know. I've got it all right." He hollered out to his secretary, "Make an appointment for me with Dr. Torro."

"I know," said Belavista. "Gets you around the back, too, a little."

"A little," Stern said. "You feel as though a baby with giant inflated cheeks is in there."

"I know, I know," said the boss. "I've got it. I'm sure I've got the same thing." He shouted to his secretary, "Make sure it's for today," and then said to Stern, "I've got it, all right. I've got the same thing."

Stern felt a tiny bit of resentment now. It was as though he had finally come up with something that Belavista, with all his millions, could not have, and yet here was the man trying to horn in on Stern and get one too, a finer and richer one. Now Belavista rose and said, "All right, here's what I'm going to do for you," and Stern felt such a thrill of excitement that he had to hold on to his boss's desk. There were those who said that Belavista was a selfish and shrewd man, but Stern had always told them, "I don't see it. He comes through. He's always been very nice to me." Stern was certain Belavista had been waiting for a moment of crisis, a special time to make certain announcements about Stern's future. And now Stern, near tears, wanted to hug him in advance and say, "Thank you. Oh, thank you."

"I'm continuing your salary," Belavista said.

"That's wonderful," said Stern. "It will ease my mind." And then he waited for the list to continue.

"For as long as it takes. I don't care if it's three weeks."

"That's really nice," Stern said. He looked with humility at the floor, as though he expected nothing more.

"You've been pretty good around here and I want to play fair with you," said Belavista. "I've thought it over, and that's the way I'm going to handle it. I'd like to chat some more, but I've got an appointment I can't break. So look, take it easy, get your mind off things, and everything around here will be all right."

"It's amazing the way something like this just happens to you," Stern said.

"That's right," Belavista said, tapping his foot, and Stern, aware that he was keeping him from doing million-dollar things, said, "I'll be rolling along now."

"OK, guy," said Belavista, and Stern left his office, the parachute blowing up big and painful inside him. Once, when someone at college had made fun of Stern for being from Brooklyn, Stern, whose father had made a little extra money at that time, enough to buy a car, had said, "My father can buy and sell you," to the boy. Now, hating his boss, he wanted to say to him, "My father can buy and sell you." If Belavista then pinned him down on the actual worth of his father, Stern would be vague and say, "He made a lot of money in the shoulder pad business."

It was late in the afternoon when Stern got back to his desk, an unsettling and nauseating time; each day at this time Stern would have to face going home and, at the end of his trip, driving past the kike man's house. He would do things, try to distract himself, talk to people and force jokes, but no matter what he did, he would eventually have to leave the safety of his office, where even Glover's pursed lips and his secretary's downbeat buttocks were comforts, and ride home to the kike man. Each night he would buy his newspaper at the station, sit among groups of hearty men, and when one named "Ole Charlie" told a

92

drainpipe anecdote, Stern would raise his head and guffaw at the punch line as though he understood, that he was riding home to a faulty drainpipe too, and that bad drainage was his major concern in life also. And then Stern would bury his head in his newspaper and turn to an important section, like maritime shipping, and look very serious, making an almost physical effort to blend in with the men alongside him, as though if he looked exactly like them, he would become exactly like them, speeding home to drainpipes and suburban pleasures. But then, as his stop grew nearer, a panic would start in his throat. The maritime section would become a blur and he would think how nice it would be to go one stop too far on the railroad and get off in a new place, where he could go to a home fully furnished with Early American chairs, a wife educated at European schools, neighbors named "Ole Charlie," and a street devoid of kike men.

At his desk now, Stern thought that perhaps tonight he would send his wife to tell the kike man to stop everything, to stop tormenting him, because Stern now had an ulcer. He was not ever to hit Stern in the stomach and do anything to his family, because you don't do those things to a man if he's got an ulcer. Not if you wear veteran jackets and fly flags from every window. You're a man of fair play. Stern imagined the man hearing the ulcer news and muttering something, perhaps snickering wetly; but he would never fling Stern's wife down again and peer between her legs. You don't do that to a man's wife if he has an ulcer blooming in his belly and you're supposed to be American and fair. Stern thought how much better it would be if he had lost a leg or gone blind. Then the man would certainly never do anything to him again. If he were blind, that would be complete protection for Stern's wife and child. At a meeting, the man might tell with a giggle of the blind Jew in the neighborhood, but it would be hands off Stern's wife and child. Perhaps, though, Stern had it all wrong. Perhaps the man's commando training would prevail. Never give up an advantage. If you blind a man, but there is still life inside him, jump on him and snuff it out. And Stern imagined himself tapping sightlessly past the man's house, his wife and child flanking him. The man would spot them, walk slowly forward, then gather some speed, put Stern out of commission with a judo chop, kick his child in the crotch, and then get his wife down to stab her sexually, and, worse, get her to wriggle and whimper with enjoyment beneath her conqueror while Stern thrashed blindly in the street.

Stern sipped milk now, got his desk in order, and thought of leaving the container in the center of his desk so that others would find it the following day and be consumed with heartbreak at the tragic symbol. At his desk, Glover spoke with pursed lips to the Board, and Stern imagined suddenly with fright that the moment he left for Fabiola's rest home, Glover would resign from the Board, renounce all effeminate mannerisms, marry immediately, and move into a split-level, thereby becoming attractive to Belavista. When Stern returned, his ulcer vanquished, Glover would be sitting at Stern's desk.

Stern's one Negro friend, Battleby the artist, came in then with sketches for Stern's labels and began immediately to fill Stern in on all his latest activities. A bearded Negro intellectual, he behaved as though his paintings were the major concern of all Americans and people walked the streets in a sweat, chafing to get late details on his career. When someone else in a room was speaking, Battleby felt threatened and would sweat and fidget, tugging at his collar and gulping deeply for air until the person stopped; then Battleby would swallow deeply and say, "They have some pen-and-inks of mine over at the

West Side Gallery, and a Guggenheim director said I'm one of the eight best young Americans in casein."

Battleby sat down now and said to Stern, "Here are the sketches. I'm doing something new with ceramics that an art editor has said promises to be one of the real technical contributions to the art world. You know my far-out comic strip? Well, the syndicate says if I can sharpen the punch line just a little, I have a good chance of selling it to them. The nudes are going quite well. I can sell almost as many as I like. I may teach a course this summer at Polytech in techniques of the French moderns."

For a moment Battleby seemed to forget his next achievement, and when Stern leaned forward to say something, a panic flew into Battleby's eyes and he began to fidget and sweat and tap his feet until he remembered and choked out the next line. "Showing. A showing. If I can come up with twenty-six canvases by September, there's a gallery on Madison that wants me. They once had an original Braque."

He plunged on in this style, and in a way Stern wanted him to continue all night, because he knew that when Battleby stopped, he would have to put on his jacket and go to the train. He wanted, though, to stop Battleby and talk to him about the kike man, but he was afraid to cut him off for fear of being thought anti-Negro. Because he was so embarrassed about his cowardice, he never really talked to anyone about the man down the street, and Battleby seemed a good person to talk to. Who could he repeat it to? A bunch of people up in Harlem? As Battleby went on about his achievements and the people who thought his work was fine, Stern wondered if he could get Battleby to stop being an intellectual for a second and tell Stern some special Negro things about kicking prejudiced people in the guts. He liked his friend's work, though he thought that Battleby used too many browns, tossing them in inappropriately for ocean scenes, and that the paintings, if inhaled, would even smell a little Negro. He had a strong interest in Battleby's work, and yet another of his reasons for having Battleby as a friend was that down deep he felt he could count on the Negro to hide him from the police in a teeming Harlem flat if ever he were to kill someone. He hoped, too, though he could never suggest this, that Battleby would one night furnish him with supple-bodied Negro girls of Olympian sexual skills who would scream with abandon when Stern bit them gently. And now, as Battleby droned on, he even dared to hope that when he told Battleby of his predicament, the Negro would fling off his horn-rims and fill an open-cab truck with twenty bat-carrying Negro middle-weights, bare to the waist and glistening with perfect musculature. Then Battleby would drive them at great speed to Stern's town to do a job on the man down the street, the pack of them entering the man's house swiftly and letting him have it about the head.

The next time Battleby paused for breath, Stern said, "I don't feel so good. I've got to go away for a while. Look, we never talk, but I've got to talk to someone. Something happened to me out where I live. A guy did this to me because I'm Jewish. You probably run into a lot of Negro things. We never talked about stuff like this before, but I thought we could now."

Battleby fidgeted on his chair and gulped for air, blinking at Stern incredulously, as if to say, "You don't understand. The conversation is about me. I talk about things that have happened to me, and I don't get into other things."

Battleby said: "I've got some crucifixion oils I'd love for you to see. Real giant things with a powerful religious quality. I don't see how I was able to come up with them."

"No, I mean it," Stern said. "I have to talk to someone.

What happened is that this guy got my wife down and looked inside her legs and she wasn't wearing anything. This is no fun for me to say, believe me. Then he said kike at her, and the worst thing is I never did anything about it. My kid was standing there. I walked over, but I didn't do anything, and now I'm sick and have to take off for a while. You probably run into a lot of Negro things like that."

A change seemed to come over Battleby now. It was as though he'd been hoping Stern would never get into personal affairs, but now that he had, he wasn't going to let his old friend down. He took off his glasses, wiped them, and began to gulp and shake his head, as though what he were about to say was so true and real he could hardly get it out. Then, in a voice that had all the patience and tolerance of an entire race of long-suffering Negroes, he said, "You have got to abstract yourself so that you present a faceless picture to society.

"We all do," said Battleby, shaking his head and replacing his horn-rims. "Every one of us do."

Stern, puzzled, but afraid that if he asked for elaboration, Battleby would find him anti-Negro, said, "All right. I'm going to start doing that thing right away."

"Good," said Battleby, rising to leave. "I'll call you as various things on me come up." And Stern, heartsick that he had not asked about the truckload of middleweights, watched the heavy-necked Negro intellectual fly down the hall.

Talking to Battleby, Stern had not thought about his stomach, but now he touched it tentatively and a cloudburst of pain washed upward from his feet and filled his ribs. It was as though a sleeping ulcer had been annoyed and now waited within him, angry, red-eyed, and vengeance-seeking. It did not seem possible that such a large mass of terribleness could be cleared up without "going in," and Stern was certain Fabiola was wrong after all. He imagined a scene in which a thin-lipped gentile surgeon would deftly slice down several layers inside him and then, after furtively looking about to see that no one was watching, reach in and pluck out fistfuls of things Stern vitally needed. The gentile would then sew him up, leaving Stern four more years of life, in order to avert suspicion.

He finished a container of milk, leaving it slightly crushed and forlorn in the center of his desk, and then walked slowly to the train station, stalling, hoping that something would happen, a minor car accident perhaps, that would eliminate his having to go past the kike man's house. Girls streamed by in the street with lovely unsettling bodies, and Stern imagined the eyes of a good one suddenly meeting his with instant understanding, the two of them going silently to her room to make love, and Stern, by the sheer violence of his thrust, passing the ulcer down through his stomach, out along his organ, and into her belly, where the girl would somehow accept it with more strength than he had been able to.

On the station platform, Stern stood next to two tall, starched, elderly men, both of whom looked like entire organizations in themselves. First one, then the other would make a hearty, obvious observation about the train system, delivered in a deep, resonant, corporational voice, and then both would chuckle with warm, folksy helplessness at the remark. When the train pulled in, leaving the car door a few feet from where they stood, one said, "Looks like that engineer went and missed us again," and the other jabbed him in the ribs and said, "He sure did," and then both laughed with heartiness. The first one said, "Guess we better get our seats before they're all gone," and the second said, "Else maybe they'll raise the price now," and then both howled and patted each other on the back.

They took seats behind Stern, and one said, "Sure gonna miss these old rides when I take m'vacation." The other said, "Gonna have yourself a little fun, are ya'?" He dug the first in the ribs, and then both slapped their knees. The train was late getting started, and Stern thought he would join in and try one of their obvious remarks. He wheeled around and said, "Looks like we'll never get out of here." The pair looked at him with hostility.

After the train started, the men began to read newspapers, one of them holding his in such a way that the edge of it cut into Stern's neck, chafing it as he turned the pages. Stern wanted to turn around and ask the man to hold it another way, but he was sure the man would rise and make a speech to the other passengers about Stern, unveiling him as a Jewish newcomer to the train, editor of sin-town stories. He would first warm up the audience, getting laughs from some obvious but folksy remarks, and then deliver his denunciatory speech with confidence and authority, as though he were speaking to a board. He would then turn the floor over to Stern, who would begin a sophisticated anecdote, get confused, and finally slink down wordlessly in his seat, the sin-town editing charge unrefuted, while other gentiles in their seats applauded derisively and shouted, "Hear, hear; fine speech." He made irritated shrugs with his neck, hoping the man would get the idea, but the paper edge remained against his neck. Stern finally wheeled around, but when his eyes caught the other man's unblinking gaze, he looked upward, as though his intention had been to examine the car ceiling.

A conductor around the same age as the two men came and stood next to them, swaying in the aisle, and one of them said to the other, "He's sure got the racket, don't he?" The second one howled and said, "Betcha he's got a little snort in his pocket for you if you ask him," and then both rocked with laughter as the conductor shook his head in mock exasperation and said, "You guys are great kidders."

It was stuffy in the train, and Stern could not get his window open. He opened his belt all the way, as though to give the ulcer more room and comfort, but it seemed to swell and spread out, as though it would occupy any amount of space it was given. Stern felt uncomfortable and remembered suddenly that Fabiola had told him always to be on the lookout for a black coffee-grounds substance if he should have occasion to vomit. This thought, combined with the stuffiness and the paper in his neck, nauseated him; he was hemmed in by a small lady who glittered blindingly with jeweled ornaments. "I think I've got to get out of here and vomit," he said to her, getting up and making his way past her knees. "Why didn't you think of it before?" she said, shifting herself in annoyance. "You're halfway there." Stern got out into the aisle and asked the conductor, "Which way to vomit?" The conductor considered the question a long time, then shook his head and began to walk to one end of the car. The two men stuck their heads in their newspapers, as though Stern had violated his twentieth rule since the trip began and was past all comment. He followed the conductor to the platform between cars. The conductor pointed to a corner of the tiny platform and said, "Vomiting's done in there on newspapers. I'll get passengers out the other way."

"Can I begin now?" Stern asked, not wishing to violate any vomiting protocol. Without answering, the conductor walked back into the car. Stern realized he had no paper and returned to the smoker, where he asked a man for some. "I'm not feeling so hot," he said, and the man said, "All righty," and gave him a section he had already looked at. Stern spread it out in the corner of the between-cars platform and tried to vomit neatly and with as little fuss as possible. It occurred to him before he started that perhaps he might vomit forth the ulcer and then kick it off the platform, rid of it forever, but then he went ahead, and when he was finished, his stomach remained bloated with pain. He searched the floor now, looking for coffee grounds, but there was no trace of any, and in a sense he felt a little disappointed. He remained on the platform with the newspapers, guarding the area, as though to prove he didn't want to evade responsibility. He remained crouched next to the newspaper, and he wondered what happened to people who died on the between-cars area. Did they have a special procedure for getting them off the train? Were they taken off on stretchers, keeping up the ruse that they were still alive, or were they simply carried off in special body bundles?

When the train stopped, the conductor diverted people in Stern's car to the other exit and then came back to Stern. "I guess you can go now," he said. "Try and do this before starting out or after getting there."

"All right," Stern said, and walked off the train, relieved that he did not have to go through a special trial for vomiters and that he was still allowed to use the train.

The sun was going down as Stern got into his car, and he wished now that there was some way to let the kike man know that this was a day in which he had just vomited and had gotten official confirmation of his ulcer and that, just for this one day, it was all to stop. He was to stop hating Stern and Stern was to be allowed to just put the man out of his mind. He was to be allowed to ride home just like any other man coming home to his family.

In a way, though, the ulcer that raged within him and the train vomiting seemed to release him and give him a tiny flutter of courage. He drove toward the man's house with the feeling that he had been given the ulcer and had vomited in humiliation on a train and now there was little else that could happen to him. Once, when Stern was young, his mother had bought a corduroy jacket for his birthday and he had worn it in the street. The orphan boy, who had tormented and bullied him for months, swept down suddenly and tore the jacket from Stern's body, slipping into it himself and then dancing around in it tantalizingly, beyond Stern's reach. A coldness had come over Stern and he had advanced toward the boy with poise and self-control and said, "Give me that jacket." The onlookers had said, "Are you crazy? He'll crack your head." But the orphan boy, startled by Stern's show of resistance, had taken off the jacket and said, "Here. Can't you take a joke?" And Stern had put the jacket back on and then slipped into the old relationship, in which the bigger and stronger boy tormented and bullied him, knocking him against buildings, blackening his eyes, picking him up, and slamming him to the ground. Now, as he drove past the man's house, the feeling of control returned for an instant and he slowed down. He thought that he would walk into the man's house, take off his coat, and say, "Just wear this coat. I dare you to wear it. My mother bought it for me." And then, if the man put on the coat, Stern would somehow be able to crush him with a blow, battering his head through his living-room window. But then Stern thought, "What if he declines to wear the coat, grins wetly, and simply drives his fist into my ulcer-swollen belly, actually breaking open a hole in it?" And so Stern drove past the man's house, his hands shaking at the wheel.

Outside his house, with the dark·coming on fast, Stern walked across the lawn, kicking furiously at fallen pears and crying through his nose. He did this for a long time, and he was not without the thought that perhaps it would help; he would be heard, someone would be touched, and when he dried his eyes, there would be no ulcer.

His wife had gone for the day, leaving the child in the care of a baby-sitter, and when Stern paid her and sent her away, he saw that his parents had driven out unexpectedly.

Stern's father was a small, meticulously dressed man whose years of cutting shoulder pads had made him terribly precise about details. Whenever Stern, as a boy, began the new side of a quarter-pound stick of butter that had been started on the other side, his father would slap his hand and say, "That's no way to do it. I can't understand you." He spent a great deal of time after meals scooping up bread crumbs with a precise rolling motion of the knife, not stopping until he had gotten every last crumb. His teeth were his best feature, and whenever he passed a mirror he would draw back his lips and try several varieties of smiles, practicing broad ones and quick, spontaneous grins. He had a special thin, six-note whistle, which Stern as a boy had always listened for late at night; it meant he was home, and Stern would watch him from the window, a small man, walking jauntily, on his way to the three-room apartment to practice a few quick grins before the mirror and then sit down to eat a meal with factorylike precision. Stern had not fancied the idea of having a small father, but one day he had seen this compactly built man point his nose up at a towering motorman on a crowded subway train and say, "Ah, button up or I'll dump you on your ass." The nose he had thrust up in the motorman's face had a jagged scar along its bridge which fascinated Stern. Whenever his father practiced grins, he would also check the scar, stretching it for a good look. Stern liked to run his finger along his father's nose scar, gently, as though it still might hurt. One day his father told Stern the scar had been given to him by two soccer players in a strange neighborhood who had suddenly lashed out and knocked him unconscious. The friends of Stern's father had gone looking for the men with steel piping but never found them. Stern liked that story and told it to people all the time, enjoying it when he could say, "My father's friends went looking for the guys with pipes." Stern wished he had friends who would do that for him.

When Stern's father had failed to inherit the shoulder pad business from his brother Henny, he had simply continued on as a shoulder pad cutter, smiling surreptitiously into mirrors, and seemed not to have realized that his whole life had gone down the drain. He did describe his brother Henny's death often, however, acting it out in vigorous pantomime. "They just found him sitting in a chair," he would tell the listener, "like this," and then he would let his knees bend a little, his arms sag at his sides, and pop his eyes, letting his tongue hang grotesquely from his mouth.

When the business dream had faded, however, Stern's mother had never recovered. It meant she could never own a home in Saint Petersburg and decorate it in Chinese modern. She had been a tall, voluptuous woman with much nerve. When Stern was young, she would just hail cars on the street instead of cabs, and then she and Stern would jump into them that way with whoever was driving. In restaurants she would grab celebrities and hold them by the sleeve, hollering across to the embarrassed young Stern, "I've got Milton Berle" or "I just grabbed Bob Eberle." After the business debacle, she aged swiftly and began to drink. She tried furiously to cling to her youth and did little dance steps all the time, humming to herself and executing them in subways, in bars, on the street. When she was with Stern in restaurants or anywhere in public, she would look at a strange young man and say, "He's for me" or "I could make him in ten seconds." Stern would answer, "I don't get any kick out of hearing things like that." The phrase "make" sickened him. He didn't want to know about his dated mother, with her slack, antique thighs and dyed hair, doing old-fashioned things with strange, dull men.

They waited in the house for him on this day, Stern's father in a slipover sweater, his mother in toreador pants, and they had brought along Stern's Uncle Babe, a thin man with giant Adam's apple who had spent much of his life in mental institutions. Married to a concert violinist and thought to be of modest circumstances, he had attended a recital one evening and run amok, certain there were poison gases in the air. When police subdued him, he was found to be carrying bankbooks showing balances of a million dollars. Stern had childhood memories of visiting him in frightening institutions, bringing him boxes of pralines, his favorites, and then seeing Uncle Babe led out in institution clothes, which were always too large. Stern would sit and smile at his uncle on a bench, and then, on the way home, his mother would say, "He has some head. As sick as he is, he can tell you smarter things than people on the outside."

Now, Stern's mother led forth Uncle Babe and said to Stern, "Look who I brought out for you. Uncle Babe. You always loved him."

Stern hugged Uncle Babe with great tenderness, as though to make up for all the wrongs done to him by heartless institutions, and Stern's mother said, "Get him to tell you about the market. To this very day, he has some head." Stern sat alongside his Uncle Babe and the

105

conversation took the usual course. Uncle Babe would make a few statements about the financial world, too generalized to be put to any moneymaking use, and then would slide into a monologue about the difficulty of getting a decent piece of fish, various smells in the air, and how certain shirt fabrics itched your skin.

"He has some head if you can only keep him on the right track," said Stern's mother.

After a while, Stern arose and said, "I can't listen to anybody any more. I've come home today with an ulcer."

Stern's mother said, "I don't believe it."

Stern said, "I've got one, all right. With a large crater. In two days I have to go to a rest place for it. It hurts right now."

"That's what I needed," Stern's mother said, puffing at a cigarette. "I don't have enough. That's the perfect extra thing I need to carry."

Stern's father, standing small and round-shouldered, shook his head gravely and said, "You've got to take care of yourself. That's what happens. I've told you that and I've told you that."

Uncle Babe leaned forward, staring widely, and said, "I like a piece of fish on a night like this, but I don't like the way it smells."

"I'm going to have a drink," said Stern's mother. "And I don't need any comments either. Do you know where I'd be if I wasn't able to take a little drink?" She swallowed some Scotch from a shot glass and said, "I don't have any reason to drink, do I? No reason in the world."

"Maybe I'll just go upstairs and lie down," Stern said. "It hurts plenty inside me."

"I'm not going to worry about it," Stern's mother said. "I can't kill myself. I've had disappointments in my life, too. Plenty of them. I could tell you plenty."

"I am not interested in people's disappointments," Stern said. "My stomach hurts me."

"All right, so I said something wrong," she said. "Look, darling, stay downstairs awhile. Maybe it'll make you feel better. Talk to your Uncle Babe. You love him. You know his head.

"Maybe we could all use a little music in our systems," she said, instructing Stern's father to bring in a small accordion he carried in the trunk of his car. As a boy, Stern had sung at home to his father's accordion playing. His voice was not bad, and his mother had once taken him to a talent agent, who'd had Stern sing into his ear and then rejected him for poor head tones. But Stern's mother was rhapsodic over his voice, and now, as Stern's father played some warm-up trills, she sank into a chair and said, "Sing for me, darling. It'll make us all feel better."

"I'm not singing anything," Stern said.

"All right, don't sing for me, sing for your Uncle Babe," she said. "He's never heard your voice, and he's come all the way out here. He'll faint when he hears you."

"Jesus," Stern said. "I'm thirty-four." But when his father played an old ballad, he began to come in with the words.

"That voice," his mother said. "The same voice. I could die."

When he reached the bridge of the song, Stern said, "I'm not doing any more of this. I told you about my stomach. Doesn't anybody realize my stomach hurts? I've got a goddamned ulcer. I have to go away to a home."

"*Don't* sing," said Stern's mother. "What am I going to do—put a bullet through my head? I only had an idea. I thought it would be good for everybody." Stern's father continued through the song, as though respecting a show-business tradition that no matter how adverse the circumstances, all numbers are to be completed. Uncle Babe leaned across to Stern's mother and said, "Listen, did you take a look at my shirt? I don't like the feel of it. It doesn't feel good on my skin."

"The crazy bastard doesn't even hear the music," said Stern's mother. "He's in a world of his own."

Stern's father wound up the ballad with an elaborate trilling effect, and then Stern's mother said, "Isn't your wife home when you have an ulcer?"

"She doesn't know about it yet," said Stern.

"She ought to be home if you're not feeling well," said Stern's father.

"I said she doesn't know. Listen, none of this is doing me any good. I'm going upstairs on the bed. I'm going to a home in a few days, and I've got to stay quiet until then. Nobody upset me about anything."

He went upstairs, and when his stomach touched the bed, it seemed to puff up with pain like great baby cheeks and he had to roll over on his back to be comfortable. A car moved into the driveway and he went to the window and saw his wife hop out, come around and kiss a man through the driver's window, and then run into the house. Stern got back into bed. She was downstairs for a while, and then she ran up the steps and knelt beside him and said, "What happened?"

"I've come up with an ulcer and there'll be some kind of institution in a few days."

"Oh, that's not so bad," she said, her great eyes wide, kissing his wrist. "You'll fix it right up in a few days."

"No, I won't," said Stern. "It's a big thing and it'll be in there for a while. I may have to be away for a long time."

She was wearing a tight jumper that hugged her flaring thighs snugly; the crease of her underwear showed through, and Stern had a sudden fear that she had just thrown on her clothes in a great hurry.

"Where were you?" he asked. "I thought you don't go anywhere out here."

"I went to a modern dance class today for the first time," she said, her eyes shimmering with warmth. "I thought it would give me an interest."

"But I've come home with an ulcer," Stern said.

"I didn't know that," she said.

"Who was the one in the car?"

"José," she said. "The instructor. He picks up the students and takes them home."

"I saw a kiss," said Stern, a slow and deadly beat beginning against his stomach walls, as though fists inside him were pleading for attention.

"Oh, that's just a thing he does, like show business. It was nothing."

"But I saw tongues," said Stern.

"No, you didn't," she said. "I can't help what *he* did. I didn't use my tongue."

"Oh my God, *then there was a tongue.*"

Stern's mother and father came up to the room, followed by Uncle Babe. All three stood in the doorway.

"That's some place for a wife to be when there's a sickness," said Stern's mother. "Out of the house." She downed a shot of Scotch and said, "And they wonder why I take a little drink."

"I'll be where I want," Stern's wife said, and his small father came forth, shoved his nose into her face, and said, "You'll be home with him."

Uncle Babe came into the room, eyes wide in the pale glare of the single bedroom lamp, and said, "I smell gas; open the window, somebody," and Stern had a picture of himself, thin and unshaven, sitting in oversized clothes on the bench of one of Uncle Babe's institutions, waiting for his son and wife to visit him, the boy carrying a box of pralines for him, his favorites. The fists within him stepped up the rhythm of their beat, and Stern began to roll from one side of the bed to the other, hands tight around his stomach, as though to keep it from falling apart. "Call Fabiola," he said in a whisper. "Tell him no two days. I've got to go tonight. Oh, please, tell him I've got to get started tonight."

Fabiola told Stern of pills that would take him through the night and said he would arrange space at the home for the following morning. Stern awakened blinking to an agonizingly warm and lovely summer day. But the summer fragrance unsettled him; on such days his son would have to stand without playmates, sucking a blanket on a barren lawn, and Stern would at some point have to stand outside and perhaps see the man a mile down the road. Dark and dreary weather made Stern rejoice, because on such days there was no shame in staying inside the house, where it was safe. Down deep at the center of him there was a small capsule of glee that he was going to the home on this day; if dark and terrible things happened then to his family, he could not be held responsible. How could he prevent them if he was away in a home?

The midnight driveway kiss nagged at him now, and he reached for his wife as though to nail her down, to stake a claim in her during his absence, to mark her, change her in some way so there would be no smoothly coordinated backseat tumbles with José during his absence. She watched him like a great-eyed fourth-grade girl, but then her eyes closed, her skin became cold, and she clung to him with a nervous, clattering whimper, doing a private, rising-up kind of thing. He went at her with a frenzy, as though by the sheer force of his connection he could do something to her that would keep her quiet and safe and chaste for two weeks, but when he fell to the side he saw with panic that she was unchanged, unmarked, her skin still cold and unrelieved.

"Can you be a man again, my darling?"

"No," Stern said. "I've got something inside me. I've got to get up to that home. Listen, can you give up that ballet thing when I'm away?"

"No, I don't want to. It's the first thing I've had."

"OK, then," he said. "But no more tongues. Can't you drive home by yourself?"

"He drives the students home. The kissing is just a show-biz thing. Can't you be a man one more time? I'm going to have to jump on a telephone pole."

"I don't want you to say things like that," said Stern.

Outside, on the lawn, it occurred to Stern that he had never seen his house during the week at this precise time of day. It was eleven in the morning, a time when he was usually at work for two hours. He had gone to work on schedule for many years, and in his mind he had felt that if he ever stopped and stayed home one day, or left his job entirely, he would die. And yet here he was, standing on the lawn, looking at his home, and he was perfectly alive. Perhaps that was it, he thought; perhaps all he had to do was to stop work for one day and see that he could live and he would not have gotten the ulcer. His son came out and said, "How long will you be away?"

"A little while," Stern said.

"I can't wait for a little while," the boy said.

"I'll be back soon."

"I can't wait till soon. Listen, do you know where we are?"

"Where?" Stern said.

111

"In God's hand; right on his pinkie, as a matter of fact."

"Who teaches him God things?" Stern said to his wife.

"The baby-sitter. She's inside."

Stern said, "She shouldn't." He wanted to go inside and tell her to discontinue the God information, but he was afraid she would come after him one night with a torch-bearing army of gentiles and tie him in a church.

Stern's wife drove the car, and as they passed the man's house down the street Stern ducked down and made himself invisible, as though he did not want the man to know of his triumph. Stern was certain that if the man knew he had put Stern in a home, he would fly a dozen flags thrillingly from every window.

On the highway, Stern watched his wife's knees, apart as they worked the pedals; he imagined her dropping him off at the home, then going immediately to a service station and allowing the attendant to make love to her while her feet kept working the pedals so that she could always say that she had driven all the way home without stopping. She pulled into the driveway of the Grove Rest Home in the late afternoon and Stern, saying goodbye, squeezed her flesh and kissed her through her dress, as though by getting in these last touches he could somehow ward off the gas station attendant.

Part Three

A giant picture of a somber, bewhiskered, constitutional-looking man hung in the reception lobby. Stern took this to be Grove himself. The lobby was a great, darkened, drafty place, and as Stern passed the picture he instinctively ducked down a little, certain that Grove, in setting up the home, had no idea people such as Stern would be applying for admission. As Stern stood before the reception desk he expected an entourage of Grove's descendants to run out with clenched fists and veto him.

A tiny, gray-haired nurse looked up at him and said, "What can I do for you, puddin'?" Stern told her who he was.

"Of course, dumplin'," she said, checking her records. "You're the new intestinal. I'll get Lennie out for you. Does it hurt much?"

Stern said he'd had a bad night and asked what the rate was. She said three dollars a day. "That includes your three meals and your evening milk and cookie."

Stern had been ready to pay ten dollars a day and felt

115

ashamed at getting it for so little. She said, "Everyone pays the same rate, crumb bun," and Stern said, "I'll donate a couch later when I get out."

A tall, handsome Negro with powerful jaw muscles came out on steel crutches, moving slowly, adjusting clamps and gears as he clattered forward. He was pushing a baggage cart, and he threw his legs out one at a time behind it, as though he were casting them for fish.

"This is Lennie," said the nurse. "You'll like him. He's a sugarplum. Lennie, this is Mr. Stern, your new intestinal."

"Very good," said the Negro. "Bags on the cart, Mr. Stern. Patients to the left of me as we walk."

"I can handle them," said Stern. The Negro's jaw muscles bunched up, and he said, "Patients to my left. Bags on the cart."

Stern, afraid of his great jaw muscles, tossed his bags on the cart, and the Negro began to clatter forward, clamps and gears turning, leg sections rasping and grinding out to the side, one at a time. Stern fell in beside him, hands in his pockets, feigning a very slow walk, as though he, too, took days to get places.

"Are you originally from New York?" Stern asked. "I just came from there and it's funny, but the last guy I saw was a Negro artist friend of mine."

"There'll be no dinner," said the Negro, sweat shimmering on his forehead as he pushed the cart, looking straight ahead. "That's at five. You're late for milk and cookie, too. One lateness is allowed on that, though. Did the nurse furnish you with milk and cookie?"

"No," said Stern.

The Negro's jaw muscles tightened again, and he glared violently at Stern. He released the cart, turned around after much shifting and switching of gears, and began to make his way back to the nurse. Stern walked several steps behind him. When the Negro got back to the reception desk, he asked the nurse, "Did you give this intestinal milk and cookie?"

"No, I didn't, old stocking," said the nurse.

"That's what he claim," said the Negro, freezing Stern with another glare. Once again he shifted gears, arranged clamps, tugged and yanked at elaborate mechanisms, and finally turned and walked complicatedly down a dark ramplike hall, Stern falling in beside him. The darkness was dropping swiftly; parallel to the ramp and off in the distance were the blinking lights of a building that seemed to be set off by itself, deliberately isolated. Crowd sounds were coming from it, as though from a bleachers group that had remained long after a ball game.

"Is that where we're going?" Stern asked the Negro.

"You're not to go there," he said. "That's Rosenkranz, where mentals are to be taken. And you're not to be social with attendants at Grove, such as myself."

He looked straight ahead as he took his zigzagging, clanking, spastic steps, and Stern was somehow convinced that this man was doing the most important work in the world. That there was nothing of greater moment than being the attendant for intestinals and being in charge of baggage carriers. Despite his complicated legs, he seemed a terribly strong man to Stern, who felt that even were he to flee to the Netherlands after a milk and cookie infraction, getting a fifteen-hour start, the Negro would go after him Porgy-like and catch him eventually. He wondered if somehow he might not be able to enlist the Negro and his great jaw muscles to fight the man down the street. He saw the man knocking the Negro down seven or eight times and the Negro disgustedly wiping off his clean intern's jacket, making clamp and

117

gear adjustments, and then, handsome face serious and determined, great jaw muscles bunched, coming on to squeeze the life out of the kike man's throat.

They came finally to the end of the ramp and to a two-story dormitory, which Lennie identified as Griggs. He pointed to a room right inside the entrance and said, "One is not ever to enter the staff room. There is to be a line outside for medicines and, later, for milk and cookie. There'll be no leaving the grounds either; otherwise, strict penalties will ensue."

Stern's room was on the second floor. It took double the usual number of gear shiftings and fastener slidings for the Negro to mount the stairs, and when he was up there his jaw muscles were lumped enormously and his white intern's jacket was soaked. Stern said, "Thank you for all your trouble," and the Negro, after opening the room door, said, "One is to obey all rules here on the premises."

Stern's room was long and thin and rancid, as though aging merchant marine bosuns with kidney difficulties had spent their lives in it. A small middle-aged man with a caved-in chest and loose pouches under his eyes sat on one of the two beds in the dim light and said, "Hey, what's this?"

"What?" asked Stern.

The man had arranged his hands in a tangled way, as though he were scrubbing them, and was holding them against a lamp so that a clumping, knobby shadow showed against the wall.

"I don't know what that is," Stern said.

"See the dingus? See the wang-wang?"

"What do you mean?" Stern asked.

"You know. It's sexeroo. Screwerino."

Stern looked at the shadows again and, as the man manipulated his fingers, Stern thought he could make out a rough picture of a pair of sexual organs in contact.

118

"That's pretty good," Stern said.

"Check these," the man said, pulling a medallion out of his T-shirt and beckoning Stern closer. Stern looked at it, a carving of a lion and a deer, which turned into a pair of male and female genitals when tilted at an angle.

"See the dingus? Can you see the wang-wang? You want to hold it and fool around with it awhile?"

Stern actually wanted to get a better look at it, but he said, "No, thanks. I'm just getting in here and I want to take it easy. I'm going to just lie down and not do anything for a while."

"I got that last set from a guy carved them in prison. Listen, do you want me to do another one on the wall? I can do blowing."

"I just want to lie down here," said Stern, "and take it easy the first night. I have some things on my mind."

Stern got down on the bed and thought again about the man down the street. He imagined coming home and finding out that the man had moved away, unable to make his mortgage payments. Or that he had developed a lower-back injury, so that the least motion would cause him agony. Stern saw himself running over with extended hand and showing the man that he would not take advantage of him, that he would not fight him in his weakened condition, that Jews forgive. He wanted opportunities to demonstrate that Jews are magnanimous, that Jews are sweet and hold no grudges. He pictured the man's boy falling down a well, and Stern, with sleeves rolled up, being the first to volunteer to work day and night digging adjacent holes to get him out. Or the man's child being stricken with a rare disease and Stern anonymously sending checks to pay the medical bills but somehow letting the man know it was really Stern. And then he saw himself and the man becoming fast friends from that point on, Stern inviting him in to the city to meet Belavista, showing the man he didn't mind his work clothes. But mostly he wanted the back injury, and clenched his fists and squeezed his eyes hard, as though just by straining he could make it happen. If only there was a way, he thought, that he could pay to make it happen—even a large figure like $8,000, which he would work off at $10 a week.

His room-mate asked, "Do you mind any farting?" And Stern said, "I don't have any views on that."

"I cut loose a few," said the man, "but I wanted to ask, because I know a lot of the younger ones object."

The room was thick with the smell of merchant marine sheets, and Stern sat up, touching his stomach to see whether it had gotten any better since he had come to the home.

"I've got something in here and I wonder how long I'm going to have to take to get it out of here," Stern said.

"I've got the weakness is all that's wrong with me," said the man. "I've had it ever since I left the circuit. I did comedy vignettes. I used to get fifty-two straight weeks in those days, but snappers killed me off and I can't work any more. You see, I never used many snappers, maybe three a night. What I'd do is work around m'crowd, futz them along a little, nurse them, slowly giving them the business, and then, maybe after twenty minutes, I'd come in with m'snapper. I'd use maybe three a night, four tops. Nowadays the new ducks throw them out a mile a minute, no futzing in between, just one after another. Anyone who books you wants you to shoot out a million snappers before he'll even consider you. Well, I just couldn't change my style, and now I've got the weakness."

"I don't know what to say to any of that," Stern said. "I'm just here to get rid of something I've got in here."

"Suck what?" said the man.

"What do you mean?" asked Stern.

"That's one of them. One of my old snappers. I'd ask a Saturday night bunch if they had any special song requests, and when they hollered out a few, I'd take my time, do a little business with m'feet, and then say to them, 'Suck what?'"

The room seemed to have gotten narrower, and Stern was afraid that someone would seal him in with the merchant marine sheets and the old actor.

"I'm just going to go out and get the feel of the place," Stern said, getting up from the bed.

Stern walked outside in the hall and got his first look at the half man. Starting with his neck and going all the way down his body, about half had been cut away. In the shadows, with a handkerchief around his neck and a violin in his hand, he made a beseeching sound at Stern. His voice seemed to come from some place a foot away from him and sounded like a radio turned on a little too loud and tuned in to a small, dying station in New Jersey. Stern walked ahead, his face frozen, as though he did not see the man, and on the way down the steps he heard an off-key violin melody played with sorrow and no skill, muffled by a closed door. Stern wondered whether at some future date, when halves started to be taken out of him, he too would be farmed off to a home to sit unloved in the shadows and play a tortured violin.

Downstairs on the front porch a scattering of people talked beneath a great insect-covered bulb. An old man, gray-haired, draped over a wooden banister like a blanket, winked deeply and called Stern forward. In the weeks to come, Stern was to see him clinging insect-like against poles, draped over rails, propped up against walls, but never really standing. Whenever the people at Griggs moved somewhere as a unit, to meals or to the outdoor stadium, the strongest would always carry Rooney, who

121

weighed very little, and see that he was perched or propped up or laid comfortably against something. His main concern was the amount of money great people had or earned, and his remarks were waspish on this subject. He poked Stern in the ribs and said, "Hey, the President don't make much dough, does he? I mean, he really has to hustle to scrape up cigarette money." He chuckled deeply and, poking Stern again, said, "You know who else is starving to death? Xavier Cugat. I mean, he really don't know where his next cuppa coffee's comin' from." He became convulsed with laughter. "He goes to one of them pay toilets, he's got all holy hell to scare up a dime. Jesus," he said, choking with laughter and poking Stern, "we wouldn't want to be in his shoes, would we? We sure are lucky not to be Cugie." He started to slip off the rail and Stern caught him and propped him up again. "Thanks, kid," said Rooney. "All them guys are starving, you know."

A tall, nervous, erupting teen-age boy was on the porch, pushing back and forth in a wheelchair a Greek youth who Stern learned had had a leg freshly cut off in a street fight. A blond nurse with flowering hips passed by and the Greek boy said, "The last day I'm going to jazz that broad. They're going to let me out, see. That's when I tear-ass up the steps and catch her on the second floor and jazz her good. I going to jazz her so she stays jazzed."

"Where are you tear-assin'?" said the tall boy. He combed his blond hair nervously with one hand as he pushed the wheelchair. "You got one leg gone."

"Shut up, tithead," said the Greek boy, concentrating hard. "I jazz her. Then they come after me and I cut out to Harlem. I cut out so they never find me."

"Where you cuttin'?" asked the tall, nervous boy. "You can't cut nowhere."

"You're a tithead," said the boy in the wheelchair.

122

Stern approached the pair and the tall, blond boy said, "How are you, fat ass? Jesus," he said to the boy in the wheelchair, "you ever see such a fat ass?"

Stern smiled thinly, as though this were a great joke and not an insult.

"I've put on a little weight because of something I've got inside me," he said. "It certainly is a lovely night."

The tall boy erupted in violence. "You trying to be smart or something?"

"What do you mean?" said Stern in panic.

"Talking like that. You trying to make fun of us?"

"Of course not," Stern said.

"What did you say lovely for? We're just a bunch of guys. The way I see it, you think maybe you're better than the rest of us."

"It's just a way to say something, is all," said Stern.

The boy was a strange mixture, exploding with rage one minute and lapsing into a mood of great gentleness the next. The latter quality took over now, and he began to pour out his thoughts, as though he might never have another chance to talk to someone so smart he used "lovely" and wasn't even showing off. It was as though the occasion called for conversation only on the highest level.

"I've got bad blood," he said, the violence gone. "I couldn't get into the Army with it. I work on high wires, you know. I'm the only one who don't use a safety harness. You know, I'll just swing from one wire to another. The guys see me, they flip out. I'm not afraid of anything. You get killed; so what? Then my blood gets lousy and I have to stay in bed three months, six months, I don't care. I just like to have freedom. A bunch of us guys was sitting around at Coney Island eating a plate of kraut and the man comes over and says it's time to close and takes away my plate of kraut. He didn't say it nice or anything. Right

123

away he's stepping on our head. So we really give it to him and run the hell out of there. I hit him with the whole table.

"But you see what I mean?" he said with an overwhelming tenderness, as though Stern were his first link with civilization and he wanted Stern to interpret his position before the world. "A guy has to have freedom. The whole trouble with everything is that there's always somebody stepping on your head when you're eating a bowl of kraut."

"Sounds pretty reasonable," said Stern.

"Are you sure you're not trying to show us up?" the boy said, erupting again and taking Stern by the collar.

"No," Stern said, imagining the boy hitting him with a table.

"You're all right," the boy said, the gentleness returning. "I'll bet the only reason you have a fat ass is because you're sick, right?"

"That's why," said Stern.

"Maybe one night—George, you, and me—we all go downtown to get some beers."

By sliding and slipping from railings to banisters, Rooney had attached himself to a pole close to the trio. "You know who don't have a pot to piss in?" he said. "The guys who run this place. They don't eat good at all, do they?" he said, chuckling deeply and clinging to the pole like a many-legged insect.

The little staff room inside the front door lit up now, and from within, behind a counter, the Negro attendant said, "Line up for bandage and pill. Staff quarters are not to be entered."

The porch people lined up outside the staff room, Rooney sliding and clinging along as the line moved. The old actor had come downstairs and was standing alongside a dark-haired woman with sticklike legs and a thin mustache. Her head was covered with a kerchief and she tittered shyly as the old actor whispered things into her ear. He was very courtly toward her, making deep, gallant bows, and Stern wondered whether he had shown her any medallions. Stern stood at the end of the line next to a paunchy, middle-aged man who introduced himself as Feldner. "You're an intestinal, I hear," the man said. "I had what you had, only now I'm in here worrying about something else. You're a pretty smart boy. I heard you say lovely to those kids. What do you do?"

"I write labels for products," said Stern.

"I worked the casinos all my life," said the man. "All over Europe, lately the Caribbean. But I was always betting on the wrong rejyme. I'd put my money on a rejyme, see, and then I'd be working a table, making my three clams a week, when bingo, a plane flies over, drops a bomb, and we got no more casino. Once again Feldner's got his money on the wrong rejyme. One rejyme in South America give me an ulcer, what you got. But now I'm worrying about something else. How'd you like to write a book about a guy who always bet his money on the wrong rejyme?"

When Stern's turn came, he saw that the Negro, inside the staff room, had taken off his intern's jacket. He had great turbulent shoulder muscles, and Stern wondered what his legs looked like, all fitted up in their contraptions.

"Bullet got me in the high ass region," he said, his back to Stern, preparing Stern's medication. "Pacific. It pinched off a nerve and caused my legs not to move."

Stern welcomed the sudden intimacy and said, "You get around fine. I never saw anyone handle things so smoothly. When I was a kid, I used to go up to the Apollo on Amateur Night in Harlem. You'd see some really fine acts there. That's where Lena started, and Billy Eckstine."

He put his foot inside the door and the Negro turned swiftly, jaw muscles pumped up with rage, and said, "There is not to be any entering of the staff room."

Stern said, "All right." He was the last one in line, and when he had swallowed his medicine, the Negro lowered the staff-room light and Stern went upstairs. On the top step the half man was waiting for him, a bandage around his neck. As Stern approached, he flung open his bathrobe in the shadows and said, "Look what they did to me," his voice coming from a static-filled car radio on a rainy night. Stern pushed by him, making himself thin so as not to touch him, closing his eyes so as not to see him, not daring to breathe for fear he would have to smell the neck bandage. He got into his narrow room and shut the door tight and wondered whether the half man would wait outside the door until he was sleeping and then slip into bed beside him, enclosing the two of them in his bathrobe. The old actor was wheezing deeply and Stern got between the damp merchant marine sheets, wondering whether Fabiola hadn't made a mistake in sending him to this place where he had to look at half men, as though to get a preview of horrors in store for him. He touched his middle and, disappointed that the great globe of pain still existed, began to pat it and knead it down, as though to hurry along the treatment. As always, his last thoughts before dropping off to a nightmare of sleep were of the man down the street. It struck him as unfair that no matter how many pills he put inside his stomach, no matter how gently he rubbed and patted it, no matter how healthy he got at the Grove Rest Home, he would still have to go home and drive past the man's house twice a day. The man would still be there to start Stern's belly swelling again. How unfair it was. Couldn't bodies of medical people be dispatched to tell the man that Stern was receiving treatment, was getting better, and he was to leave him alone and not bother his wife and child, otherwise Stern would crack with pain once more? Bodies of medical people with enforcement powers. Couldn't Grove send a group of envoys of this nature on ahead of him before he got home, so the man would know?

Stern awakened the following morning to a sweetly cool summer morning, and waiting to welcome him was the actor, standing barefooted in a great tentlike pair of old actor's underwear, sequined in places, gathering the folds of it into his stained pants, and rubbing his meager arms.

"Got to get the pee moving," he said. "What did you think of my doll? That's good stuff, boy. Gonna get me some of that stuff."

Stern said she was very nice and dressed quickly. The old actor, still rubbing his arms, said, "You ought to try this. Nothing like it to get your wang-wang in shape."

Downstairs, on the porch, the Griggs people stood around silently in the dewy morning, and when Stern and the actor arrived, they all began a dumb march to the dining room, a broken parade led by the tall, erupting boy with the boneless, insectlike Rooney in his arms. Carrying Rooney was a privilege that went to the strongest of the group. After them came the Greek boy, wheeling along furiously, saying, "Wait up, fuckers," and then the main body, followed finally by the half man, old-fashioned toothache towel around his neck, radio-croaking to the wind. In the dining room he took a table by himself. Stern sat with Feldner and a small, scowling man who kept invoking the power of his labor union. He tried a roll, found it hard, and said, "I don't have to eat a roll like that."

"Why not?" Stern asked.

"I belong to a powerful union."

Later, when his eggs were served, he said, "Union gets you the best eggs in the country."

Stern ordered some cereal. When he took a spoonful, Feldner stopped his hand and said, "You can't eat that."

"How come?" Stern said.

"Not in the condition you're in," he said. "I had what you got. You're a nice kid, but it would tear you up."

"I get to eat cereals," said Stern. He buttered some bread and Feldner said, "Are you trying to commit suicide? I told you I had what you got. I been all over the world, in every kind of country. You're in no shape to eat that."

"I have a different kind of doctor," Stern said, eating the bread but wondering whether Feldner's doctor wasn't better than Fabiola.

"There's only one thing you can eat with what you got," said Feldner.

"What's that?" Stern asked.

"Hot stew. The warm is what you need. It warms you up in there and heals everything up. The way you're eating, you're dead in a month."

"I have a doctor who says bread and cereal are all right," Stern said, but the pain ball seemed to blow up suddenly beneath his belt and he wondered whether to call Fabiola and check on stew.

At the next table, the old actor made courtly, charming nods at the mustached stick woman. When she turned to blow her nose, he stuck a fork up through his legs, poked Rooney, who clung to a chair next to him, and said, "Hey, get this wang-wang."

At Stern's table the sullen, scowling man said, "They don't take oddballs in my union. Any crap and out you go." Finishing his meal, Feldner patted his lips and said, "You better be careful, kid. I know what you got in there.

128

You can't go eating shit. You get the hot of a stew in there and you'll see how nice it feels. I know. I'm worrying about something else, but I had what you got."

At the meal's end, the half man, who had sat alone, eating swiftly and furtively, got to his feet and began to gather everyone's dirty dishes and stack them in piles.

"It's always the worst ones who are the nicest," said the plump dining-room waitress. "It was that way at Mother Francesca's, too." Stern had been aware of the half man eating alone, had felt his eyes, and at one point had been compelled to go and sit with him, staring right at his neck bandage and saying, "Don't worry. I'll sit with you. In fact, I'll stay with you until the last half is taken away." He felt that maybe if he sat with the half man, someone would sit with *him* later, when he himself began losing halves. But on his way out of the dining room, when the half man looked up at him, he ran by frightened, as though he didn't see him.

Outside, the old actor grabbed him and, pointing to the mustached woman up ahead, whispered, "I'm going to get me some of that. That's real sweet stuff. You got to work it slow when you're handling one of them sweet dolls."

Stern stayed five weeks at the Grove Rest Home, and during this period the pain balloon that had crowded tight against his ribs began to recede until he was able to fasten the snaps of his trousers around his great girth. On some mornings during these weeks he would awaken and for an instant feel he was at the New Everglades, a mountain resort where he often spent summers as a child with his mother. Those summers days he would get up early and run down to cut a purple snowball flower for his mother to wear, wet and glistening in her hair, at the breakfast table. They were lazy, wicked times, and since he was the only young boy at the resort, he spent them among young women, playing volleyball with them, doing calisthenics, and staring fascinatedly at the elasticized garments they kept tugging at as the material crept below their shorts line. Afternoons he would lie in the bottom of a boat while his great-breasted mother, wearing a polka-dotted bathing suit that stared at him like a thousand nipples, rowed across the narrow resort river to the hut of a forest ranger who lived in the woods opposite the resort all year long. Stern hunted mussels in the shallow river water alongside the hut, and when his mother emerged from the hut she would say to him in the boat, "A hundred girls at the hotel and I'm the only one can make him." To which Stern answered, "I don't want to hear anything like that." Later, in the afternoon, Stern would sit at the resort bar with his mother, taking sips of her drink while his mother told the bartender, "That doesn't frighten me. I'll give him a little drink at his age. It's the ones that don't get a little drink from their mothers you have to worry about."

The men around his mother at the bar told dirty jokes to her, and one afternoon one of them, holding his palms wide apart and parallel, said, "Baby, my buddy here has one this long, so help me." His mother folded up with laughter on her barstool, and Stern, suddenly infuriated, hit the man in the stomach to protect her. His mother pulled him back and said, "You can't say things to his mother. He'll kill for her." Later, getting ready for dinner, Stern's mother would take him into the shower with her and he would stare at the pathetic, gaping blackness between her legs, filled with a terrible anguish and loss. Then he would rush down to cut another flower for her and, in the coolness of the evening, begin to feel very lush and elegant, as though no other boy in the world was having as wicked and luxurious a time as he, the only boy in a grown-up resort. His mother would tell him, "You're growing up too fast. You know more than kids ten years older than you." And later in the year, at school, Stern would tell his friends, "Boy, do I know things. Did I see things this summer. My mother isn't like other mothers. She just doesn't go around acting like a mother." And yet, with all the panty glimpses on the volleyball court and the barroom sips of drinks, the dirty jokes and the nervous showers, what did he actually know? It remained for a busboy in back of the resort kitchen to tell him about the sex act. Stern couldn't believe the actual machinery and said, "Really?" and the busboy said, "Yeah. When you put it in them, they get a funny feeling up their kazoo."

The Grove Rest Home had the sweet summer coolness and the proper fragrance, but it was a parody of a resort, with all its facilities torn and incomplete. Stern heard there was a small golf course and borrowed clubs one morning, setting out to look for it. He tramped the length of the institution and finally spotted a flag in the center of some tall weeds far beyond the kitchen. A bald man with a thick mustache stood alongside the single hole of the golf course, hands locked behind his back, puffing out his cheeks and flexing an artificial leg in the style of a British colonel surveying a battlefield. He said he was an electrician. A hot wire had fallen on his leg and sheared it off. His main difficulty had been in dealing with his grown son, who couldn't get used to having a one-legged father. "I told him you get older, these things happen, but he wouldn't buy it and kept spitting on the floor." The man spoke with a thick Brooklyn accent, but when he was silent, flexing his leg, he took on an amazingly autocratic demeanor, a British colonel once again. "Are you playing?" Stern asked him. "No, I'm just standing next to the hole here."

The golf course was a broken, one-holed, weeded one,

and Stern's days at the Grove Rest Home seemed weeded and broken, too. There were no scheduled activities, and between meals Stern passed the time in the library, reading peripheral books, ones written by people who had been close to Thomas Dewey and others about Canada's part in World War II. The only newspaper available was a terrible local one devoted almost entirely to zoning developments, but Stern waited for it eagerly at the front door each night, pacing up and down until it came. He looked forward, too, to "milk and cookie" each evening at seven, which was the nearest thing at the Home to a special treat. One night, when he was in line for his refreshment, the mustached woman squatted down on the front porch and began to urinate, throwing her kerchiefed head back and hollering, "Pisscock, pisscock." Gears clanking and grinding and seemingly slower than ever, Lennie came out from the staff room and made for her, finally getting there and carrying the woman, screaming, up to her room. Later, Stern learned she had been taken to Rosenkranz. In the room that night, the old actor said, "I really liked that doll. She was sweet stuff, I mean really sweet. Too bad she got the mentals. When she gets out of here, I'm going to get me some of that stuff, you wait and see."

Most of the climactic events at Grove seemed to take place on the porch during "milk and cookie." Another night, the scowling union man, two places ahead of Stern, fell forward and died. The patients made a circle around him, as though he were "it" in a sick game, and Rooney hollered, "Give him mouth-to-mouth." Afraid he would be called upon to do this, Stern said, "I'll get someone," and ran wildly into the field beyond the building, making believe he was going through the proper procedure for handling recent deaths. He came back after a few minutes to look at the union man on the floor. It was the first dead person Stern had seen, and the man did not look sweet and peaceful, as though he were asleep. He looked very bad, as though he had a terrible stomach-ache. No one had done anything yet, and the half man was now standing in the circle, croaking, "See what happens. See." It was as though he was allowed to stand with the others only on occasions such as this, a thing he knew all about. Finally Lennie arrived, stern and poised, and leaned over the man. "This is a death," he said coolly, and Stern thought to himself, "Why did Fabiola send me here? How can I possibly be helped by seeing guys dying and half men? He made a mistake."

Yet, despite the wild urination and the curled-up dead man, Stern's pain diminished gradually. Sometimes, when he sat in the fields on endlessly long afternoons, waiting for the days to pass, he would probe his middle cautiously, as though he expected to find that the ulcer had only been playing dead and would leap out at him suddenly, bigger than ever. But the circle of pain had grown small and Stern thought how wonderful it would be if the kike man was getting smaller too, if when he got back to his house, he could find the man completely gone, his house erased, all traces of him vanished, as though he'd been taken by acid or never existed.

One morning, late in Stern's stay, word spread that two industrial teams were coming to play baseball for the patients at the Home. There was much excitement, and Stern felt sorry for those shriveled people whose only fun had been at YMCA's and merchant marine recreation parlors. Not one had ever seen *My Fair Lady,* and it was small wonder they looked forward with such delight to a clash between two industrial teams. In early evening, the night of the game, Stern took his place in the dumb march formation and walked to the field, poking his belly and feeling around for the pain flower. It had been replaced by a thin, crawling brocade of tenderness that seemed to lay wet on the front of his body and was a little better than the other. But he wondered whether the ulcer might not roll forth in a great flower once again, at the first trace of friction, and then he would have the two, the flower and the brocade. He was aware that in just a few days he would have to go back to the kike man. What would happen if he merely drove by once, saw the man's great arms taking out garbage cans, and felt the flower instantly fill his stomach, one glimpse wiping out five weeks at the Grove Rest Home? And what if it went on that way, five weeks at Grove, one glimpse at arms, another five weeks at Grove, arms, until one day the flower billowed out too far and burst and everything important ran out of him and there was no more?

Stern walked behind the tall, sputtering, explosive boy, who led the march with Rooney in his arms. "You know who we ought to take up a collection for?" Rooney asked Stern as the Rest Home people took seats in the front row of the small grandstand.

"Who's that?" asked Stern.

"Yogi Berra," cackled Rooney. "I understand he's down to his last thirty-five cents." The tall boy poured him onto a bench in the front row and he clung gelatinlike to it, saying, "That Berra doesn't make ten bucks the whole season," and shaking with laughter. Stern sat between the tall, erupting young boy and Feldner. The boy, who was alternately nice and violent to Stern, asked him, "Did you ever play any ball before you picked up all that ass fat?"

"A little bit," Stern said. "And I'm not that heavy back there." He was afraid of the boy's sudden eruption and wondered why the boy couldn't be nice to him all the time. Violence was such a waste. It didn't accomplish anything. Stern had to worry that the boy would suddenly erupt and push him through the grandstand seats, maybe snapping his back like wood. He wanted to tell the boy, "Be nice to me at all times and I'll tell you things that will make you smart. I'll lend you books and, when we both get out, take you to a museum, explaining any hard things."

One of the teams represented a cash register company and the other a dry cleaning plant, and as they warmed up, the old actor ran out onto the field, stuck a bat between his legs, and hollered to the grandstand, "Hey, get this wang-wang. Ain't she a beaut?" A tall, light-skinned, austere Jamaican Stern thought might have been a healthy-legged brother of Lennie was the umpire, and he thumbed the actor back into the stands, saying, "Infraction," and then folded his arms and jutted his chin to the sky, as though defying thousands.

In the stands, Feldner, in a bathrobe and slippers, shoulders stooped from years of bending over crap tables, said to Stern, "We had softball games when I was working under one of the Venezuela rejymes. You know how long that rejyme lasted? Four days. I really backed some beauties. That's how I got what you got."

Stern felt sorry for Feldner in his bathrobe, a man whose shoulders had grown sad from so many disappointments, and wanted to hug him to make him feel better. Once, Stern's mother, infuriated at having her clothing allowance cut down by his father, had gone on a strike, wearing nothing but old bathrobes in the street. This had embarrassed Stern, who had turned away from her each time she had walked past him and his friends. Now Stern wanted to embrace Feldner as though to make it up to his mother for turning his back on her saintlike bathrobed street marches.

Stern watched the men on the two teams pepper the ball around the field and then looked at them individually, wondering if there were any on either team he could

135

beat up. They all seemed fair-skinned and agile, and Stern decided there were none, until he spotted one he might have been able to take, a small, bald one playing center field for the cash register team. But then a ball was hit to the small player and he came in for it with powerful legs churning furiously and Stern decided *he* might be too rough, also. He imagined the small, stumplike legs churning toward him in a rage and was sure the little man would be able to pound him to the ground, using endurance and wiriness and leg power.

A black-haired Puerto Rican girl came to sit with the tall, erupting, blond boy. She helped a nurse take care of a group of feebleminded children connected to the Home and Stern had seen her with a pen of them, doing things slow-motion in the sun. From a distance she seemed to resemble Gene Tierney, but up close he saw that she was a battered Puerto Rican caricature of Gene Tierney, Tierney being hauled out of a car wreck in which her face had gone into the windshield. She did things slow-motion, in the style of the retarded children she helped supervise. Sitting on the ground in front of the tall, blond, fuselike boy, she said, " You promised we were goin' dancin'."

"Shut your ass," the tall boy said. "Hey, you want to hear one? Two nudists, man and a broad, had to break up. You know why? They were seein' too much of each other."

The Puerto Rican girl giggled and leaned forward in slow motion to tickle the tall boy. Stern saw her as a Gene Tierney doll manhandled by retarded children in temper tantrums, then mended in a toy hospital.

"Your sense of humor is very much of the earth," she said.

The tall boy introduced Stern to the girl. "This is Mr. Stern," he said. "He's a swell guy, even though he's got a fat ass. I'm sorry, Mr. Stern; only kidding. He's really a good guy. Real smart.

"Listen to this one," the boy continued. "I know a guy who was invited out by Rita Hayworth. He was in her house at the time." The tall boy erupted with laughter and the Puerto Rican girl tickled him again in slow motion. Turning to Stern, she said, "He's a natural man. I'd like to feel his energy coursing through my vitals." In the distance, Stern had imagined her hips to be flaring and substantial, but actually they had a kind of diving, low-slung poverty about them. She wore a skintight blue skirt, and Stern wondered whether she hadn't worn it for an entire year and was to wear it the next three until poverty-stricken Puerto Rican underwear came bursting through its fabric. Still, the combination of Latin eroticism and intellect flashes appealed to him. It was a painful thought, and he actually gritted his teeth as it came to him, but he had to allow it to come through. This tattered Puerto Rican watcher of feeb kids was probably smarter than his wife, close to what he'd really wanted. She probably knew undreamed-of, exotic Puerto Rican love tricks. He could bring her lovely sets of underwear, tighten up some of her poetic allusions, and make her the perfect wife. He wished she was tickling him instead of the tall boy. Stern smiled at the girl. He wanted to tell her he knew better jokes, smooth situational ones, and if only she gave him a fair chance, several days of intensive conversation, she would see he was a better bet than the tall, corny boy. But he felt very old and heavy and was unable to speak.

"Got another," said the sputtering, fuselike, blond boy. "Would you rather be in back of a hack with a WAC or in front of a jeep with a creep?"

The girl dug her fingers hungrily into his ribs, saying, "You promised we'd go dancin'."

"Eat shit," the tall boy said, brushing her aside. "You know," he said to Stern, "I was once in bed for eight months. My kid sister took care of me in a little room just

137

big enough for the two of us. Every once in a while my veins give out and I can't do anything. I don't give a shit. You live, you live; you die, you die. Only thing I care about is freedom and old guys not pushing you around."

The game had begun now, and the wheelchaired Greek boy had maneuvered himself alongside the bench in the front row. He stuck his hand under the Puerto Rican girl's dress and she cringed back against the tall, grenade-like youth, saying, "I intensely dislike duos." Stern wondered what would happen if he went under there, too. He envied the wheelchaired boy. He'd gone under and nothing had happened. He hadn't been hauled off into court.

The Greek boy stared out at the cash register company pitcher and said, "He's a crudhead. I could steal his ass off. He makes one move to pitch and I'm on third like a shot."

"What are you gonna do?" said the tall boy. "Crawl on your balls?"

"Shut up, tithead," said the Greek boy.

Feldner nudged Stern and said, "I used to like baseball, but there was only one rejyme ever let us play." Then he hollered out, "Swing, baby, swing; you can hit him, baby," as though to demonstrate to Stern his familiarity with the game.

"See," he said, and Stern wanted to take him around and soothe him for being a bathrobed failure who was worried about a mysterious new something inside him.

Sitting in the grandstand now, feeling Feldner's warm, bathrobed bulk against him, Stern, despite the tender sheet that lay wet against the front of his body, felt somewhat comfortable and took a deep breath, as though to enjoy to the fullest the last few days before his return to the kike man. He was afraid of the charged and sputtering boy on his left, afraid that in a violent, pimpled, swiftly changing mood he might suddenly smash Stern back through the grandstand benches. Yet, despite the grenadelike boy, Stern still felt good being at a ball game among people he knew, broken as they were. He had cut himself off from people for a long time, it seemed, living as he did in a cold and separate place, and he thought now how nice it would be if all these people were his neighbors, Rooney in a split-level, Feldner next door in a ranch, and the old actor nearby in a converted barn. Even the half man would not be so bad to have around, living out his time in an adjacent colonial until the last half was taken away. All of them would form a buffer zone between Stern and the man down the street. That way, if the kike man ever came to fight him on his lawn, his neighbors would gather on the property and say, "Hands off. He's a nice guy. Touch him and we'll open your head."

Late in the game, a line drive caught the little bald cash register outfielder in the nose and he went down behind second base with a great red bloodflower in the center of his face. There were no substitute ballplayers, and the austere Jamaican umpire, flipping through the rule book, said, "Forfeit," jutting his chin toward the grandstand, as though ready to withstand a hail of abuse.

"I'll run that coon the hell out of here," said the wheelchaired Greek, waving his fist. "I come to see a ball game."

"That's right," said the tall boy, pimples flaring, beginning to ignite. Suddenly, his face softened. He grabbed Stern's collar and shouted, "We got someone. This guy here will play. Don't mind his fat ass." To Stern, he said, "I didn't mean that. I know you can't help it." He turned to the Puerto Rican girl and said, "Hey, a man brings home a donkey, see. So all day he goes around patting his ass."

The girl smiled, showing salt-white teeth with only the tiniest chip on a front one. She lay back, putting her head on the tall boy's lap and waggling a leg lazily, so that a gleam of Puerto Rican underwear caught the sunlight. "Boredom and you are ever enemies," she said to the tall boy. "Please sneak out and take me dancin'." The others in the stands were cheering for Stern now, and he stood up, afraid the tall boy's pimples might sputter into violence again and also not wanting to hurt anyone's feelings. It was easy to just start trotting out toward the field. He fully expected to turn back with a big smile and say, "I'm not going out there. Not when I'm sick." But he found himself jogging all the way out to center field, unable to get himself to return. Winded, he stood in a crouch, hands on knees, as though capable of fast, dynamic spurts after balls. He hoped the Puerto Rican girl was watching and would see him as being potentially lithe and graceful, equal to the tall boy. Feldner ran out in his bathrobe and slippers and said, "Do you know what will happen to you? With what you got? You play and you're dead in a minute and a half."

Stern motioned him back, saying, "I'm not sure I have what you had. Everyone's got a different kind of thing." But when Feldner turned away, discouraged, Stern was sorry he had been harsh to a man in a bathrobe.

From the stands, Stern heard the Greek boy shout, "You show 'em, fat ass," and Stern hoped the girl would not think of him only as a man with a giant behind. The austere Jamaican umpire checked Stern, looked at his rule book, said, "Legalistic," and turned stoically toward the wind.

The second hitter hit a pop fly to short center field, and Stern, since childhood afraid to turn his back and go after balls hit past him, joyfully ran forward and caught the ball with his fingertips, so thrilled it had been hit in front of him he almost cried. He did a professional skip forward and returned the ball to the infield, wishing at that mo-

140

ment the kike man was there so he could see that Jews did not sit all day in mysterious temples but were regular and played baseball and, despite a tendency to short-windedness, had good throwing arms.

A sick, reedlike cheer came from the torn people in the grandstand after Stern's catch. At the end of the inning, he trotted toward the dugout and heard the Greek boy say, "Nice one, fat ass, baby," but he averted his eyes with DiMaggio-like reserve and sat on the cash register team's bench. Feldner came over in his bathrobe and said, "What did I tell you?"

"What do you mean?" said Stern.

"Look at yourself. You should see your face."

"I look all right," said Stern. "And I'm playing now." Sitting among the lean, neutral-faced cash register team, he was ashamed of Feldner's bathrobed presence and motioned him away. But, as Feldner left, Stern again regretted his curtness and wanted to shout, "Come back. You're more to me than these blond fellows."

Stern got to bat in the inning. Afraid the dry cleaning pitcher had discovered his Jewishness and planned to put a bloodflower between his eyes, too, he swung on the first pitch, hitting it on the ground. Forgetting to run, he stood on the base path and actually squeezed with his bowels, hoping the ball would get past the third baseman. When it filtered through the infield for a hit, Stern hollered "Yoo" and ran to first, sending home the runner in front of him and tying the score. His team won in that inning and the patients gathered round him on the field. "You clobber their ass, baby," said the Greek boy with genuine sincerity, reaching up from the wheelchair to pat Stern's back. The tall boy, with gentleness in his lips, the ticking in him fading, said, "No fooling, you get around good. I mean, for a guy with a can like yours." The Puerto Rican

141

girl, still lying on the bench with gaping skirt, said, "We're all goin' dancin' tonight. Either alfresco or in my place. The group has much charm." Only Feldner had misgivings. "You signed your death warrant out there," he said, and for a moment Stern felt a bubble tremble outward inside him; he was certain he was going to have to pay for his indiscretion by starting from scratch with a brand new ulcer, slightly larger and a fraction more formidable than his first. But the bubble fluttered and withered, like a wave breaking, and the patients kept congratulating him. He had struck a blow for sickness. As a reward he got to carry Rooney back to the porch for evening "milk and cookie."

Late that night, the tall, blond boy and the wheelchaired Greek came for Stern as he sat alone on the porch. The others had gone to bed and the tall boy said, "We're meeting the kid with the boobs on the outside tonight. I figure we get a few beers and, later, diddle her boobs."

"I take her upstairs and do some jazzing," said the boy in the wheelchair.

Stern, flattered at being selected by the two, and not really sure how to say no, got up from his chair, giddy and dangerous in the night. The trio started down the corridor and then heard Lennie rasping and clattering after them, a man with a machine shop going full blast below his waist.

"There is to be no disobedience of the nighttime rules," he said, and, as the boys turned to face him, Stern wondered which side he would be on in a fight. He imagined Lennie standing against the wall, looking patiently at Stern, while the tall boy bent his contraptions and tore out his clamps and gears and the Greek boy hit him many times on the head to no avail. Stern pictured himself watching this, frozen to the side, asking Lennie, "Do you need any help?" And then Lennie, his machinery mangled, finally turning from Stern with great calm and slowly rising up, trunklike and great-armed, to hug the breath out of the two boys, subduing them for the night.

As it was, the Greek boy merely wheeled around, saying "Coon fucker" under his breath, and the tall boy, with great sweetness, said, "We were just being happy with Mr. Stern for getting a hit with a fat ass."

The two boys returned to the dormitory, and as Stern walked after them, the Negro stopped him and said, "There can be a little staying up later sometimes. If authorities come, though, I didn't see you."

Stern said, "Thank you," but he felt very uncomfortable about the favor and wanted to do a thousand quick ones for the Negro. He wanted to tell him that if he ever got into trouble with the police, he could hide in Stern's house, or if he ever wound up helpless and drugged on Welfare Island, Stern would go take a taxi in the middle of the night and cut through red tape to get him into a decent hospital. But the Negro clattered off in a metallic symphony and Stern sat guiltily on a chair, staring off at the winking lights of Rosenkranz. He stayed up late, sucking in the dewy air, exulting in its freshness, aware there were only a few days before his return to the kike man and yet thrilled that there were those few days. He wished that he were clever enough to stretch his mind so that he could turn those days into eternities, fondling each second, stretching it, cramming a lifetime into it before yielding it selfishly for the next one. Perhaps if he stayed on the porch and stared at the night, pinned it with his eyes, he would be able to hold it there and forever block out daylight. Across the field he studied Rosenkranz and wondered whether at some future date he might not himself be taken there, ulcer-free but a mindless urinator now, squatting beside the others, filling the corridors with a giant stream and cackling at the walls.

The following night, the three evaded Lennie and dashed drunkenly at midnight across the lawn toward the main gate, the tall, blond boy propelling the Greek ahead, as though the wheelchaired youth were a wild street hoop. "We meet that coon fucker tonight," said the Greek, his vehicle skidding across the wet grass, "he and me going to tangle asses." Stern kept looking back over his shoulder at the main building, as though he were a child running away from home, taking one giddy step and then another but always remaining close enough to dash back and say he was only fooling. He wondered what punishment Lennie would mete out if they were caught—and could he protest it to a higher authority without appearing to be anti-Negro? If Lennie made him stay in his room, for example. Since there were only a few days left, he would probably stay in there and let it go without fuss.

The tall boy suddenly released the wheelchair and flicked his body to the top branches of a tree like a whip, swinging easily in the wind. "Aren't I a crazy bastard?" he said from above. "That's what the guys said when I was working on high wires. I never used a safety harness. I don't care if I fall down and break my head." He swung from branch to branch like a lean night animal and the Greek boy said, "I'm cutting out. I don't want to do no stuff on trees. I want to do some jazzing."

"How you going to get up here?" said the tall boy. "With your bony ass?"

Stern wanted to tell him not to make fun of the young Greek's missing leg, but the tree swings had intimidated him and he had no desire to run up against the tall boy's explosive wiriness. Dropping easily to the ground, the tall

144

boy flung the wheelchair on ahead of him and said, "Did you see me up there? Aren't I one helluva crazy bastard? I don't care what happens to me."

Stern said, "You were very good up there," and the boy said, "But sometimes everything stops in me. I lay in bed for six months and I can't get out. My kid sister brings me soup. It's in my veins. That's what I'm in here for."

There were no guards at the gate, but as they rolled toward it, Stern had a sudden fear that Lennie had been watching them all along; the instant they passed the gate, he would have them picked up in trucks and initiate punitive measures.

"They don't like you to go through this gate," Stern said, but the Greek boy, wheeling right through, said, "I got to hop on something. Then I'm happy." And Stern raced along after the pair. The three of them traveled seven blocks in darkness, and when they came to a small bar and grill the blond boy said, "I can taste that brew already. I can't go no more than a few days without a few brews." The Puerto Rican girl was waiting for them in a booth, and it seemed to Stern that she was more like Tierney than ever, Tierney after a session with two long-shoremen who'd been paid to rough her up a little, not to kill her but to change her face around a little. She wore a bulging black sweater, and her paper-white teeth were chipped a little. Stern, drunk with the danger of having run away from the Home, wondered what her teeth would be like on sections of his body; perhaps they would nibble erotically at him in the style of some primeval creature of the Puerto Rican rain forests.

"And so ends my solitude," she said as the blond boy slid in beside her.

Stern, a weakened, dropping, off-balance feeling coming over him as a result of her literary flourish, took a seat across the table. The Greek boy swung close, chewing on his nails, examining the chrome and red leather décor. "This place stinks," he said. "We got better places in East Harlem."

"Get this," said the blond boy, poking the girl in the ribs and winking at Stern. "You know what a kiss is? An upper persuasion for a lower invasion." The girl pecked at his ear with her chipped teeth and said, "Forever play the jester." The proprietor, a tall, toplike man who looked out on the street as he spoke, came over and asked, "What'll it be?"

"We're just in here nice," said the blond boy. "We came in here nice and all we want to do is drink nice. Nobody bothers us, we don't bother nobody. Right, Mr. Stern? Didn't we come in here nice?"

"Yes," said Stern, smiling at the man, feeling the air charge up and wanting to stop whatever was about to happen. The brocade of tenderness appeared suddenly to girdle his stomach. He was not sure he could take any trouble, and he imagined himself collapsing and having to be carried back to the Home by his two friends, the Puerto Rican girl walking contemptuously behind, aware now that Stern had the least romantic disease of all.

"Brews all around," the blond boy said, his mood suddenly sweetening. When the proprietor returned to the bar, the blond boy squeezed the girl's breasts and said, "How they hangin', doll?"

"Hey, George—motorboat," he said, waggling his head from side to side against her breasts and making a droning sound in his throat.

"I don't go for that," said the Greek boy, eating deep down on his nails and leaning forward on his wheelchair, as though watching a tense horse race. "I like to do some real jazzing."

The girl sat patiently through this, running her fingers through the blond boy's hair. "The physical side," she said to Stern, who nodded back at her, his heart in his throat, as though he too considered breast-nuzzling a bore.

The proprietor brought the beers and said, "Pay now." The blond boy said, "Remember what I said when we came in? I said we're coming in here nice. Nobody pushes us around, we don't do any bumping either. Now you come over and you say pay now."

"It's a house rule," said the proprietor, staring out the window. "Everybody pays now." Stern, the brocade tightening around his stomach and wanting to do something, put down two dollars and the proprietor took it. The Greek boy said, "You think you got such a hot place here. This place stinks." He spit on the floor and the proprietor went back to the bar.

"That's what I was telling you," the blond boy said to Stern with a pleading compassion in his voice. "Nobody gives you freedom. You come into a place nice, you know, and you just want a few brews, and look what happens."

"He thinks just because he's got a fancy place he can give you shit," said the Greek boy. "I spit on his ass."

The blond boy's mood suddenly changed and he took hold of one of the girl's breasts again. "Good set, huh, Mr. Stern?" And Stern nodded sweetly in agreement, looking apologetically at the girl, as though he was only going along with this line of conversation to be polite and really never thought of such things.

"What about the dancin'?" the girl asked, looking over at the jukebox. "Does my love feel a tango within him?"

"Dancing, shit," said the blond boy. He looked over at the proprietor, who was rinsing glasses, and said, "He comes over here again, we get him. You can be nice up to a certain point."

"He thinks he has a fancy place," said the boy in the wheelchair. "I'll cut his balls."

Stern, his stomach pumping, wanted to say, "Wait. No

147

fighting. You have other things, but I have an ulcer, the kind of thing you shouldn't get excited with. What if I get hit in it and get another new one?" When the proprietor came over to the table, the blond boy arranged his fingers like two donkey's ears and stuck them swiftly in the man's eyes. The proprietor said, "I can't see now," holding his eyes, and the Greek boy grabbed his hair and yanked the man's head down on his lap, saying, "I ought to cut your balls." Then he held the man by the hair in a bent-over position and the tall, blond boy began to kick at the man's upper legs, the kicks making sharp, fresh cracking sounds, like new baseballs off a bat. Stern, who had stood by doing nothing, wanted to say, "Stop, you're going too far. The hair stuff wasn't so bad, but now you can do spinal injury." But a current began snapping through him and he looked for something to do. There was one other person in the bar, a small man with a toothbrush mustache who was eating a heavy soup. Stern ran over and grabbed him from behind, pinning his arms.

"I'm not in this," said the man.

"That's all right," said Stern, ecstatic over being in the fight, his stomach free and easy. How wonderful it would be, he thought, if he could be transported in this very condition to the kike man's front porch, the current snapping through him, the same excited sweat in his arms. He was certain he would be able to fight him and not feel a single blow, and for an instant he thought of jumping in a cab and speeding back to his house, gritting his teeth to preserve the mood. The cab fare would be $150 or so, but it would be worth it. But what if the current then began to fade, the sweat dry up, and he found himself nearing the man's house with a growing fright, worrying about being hit in the ulcer? He saw that he would have to get there instantaneously or it would not work.

After many kicks, the proprietor said, "That's enough,"

148

and the blond boy, as though waiting for him to signal with those very words, said, "Let's cut," shoving his wheelchaired friend through the door. Stern said, "I'm letting you go now," to the mustached soup eater and ran out the door after the girl, looking back at the proprietor. He was relieved to see that the man was standing; it seemed to him that only when people were on the floor might there be police involvement. The quartet ran through blackened, neatly shrubbed residential streets, and Stern wondered how running was for the ulcer. Would jogging up and down disengage it and cause it to take residence in another part of him? He was suddenly struck by the incongruity of the quartet—a grenadelike, blond boy with strange vein problems; a wheelchaired Greek; a heavy Jew with ulcer-filled stomach; and a strange, Tierney-like girl who spoke in literary flourishes. And yet they were comrades of a sort and he was glad to be with them, to be doing things with them, to be running and bellowing to the sky at their sides; he was glad their lives were tangled up together. It was so much better than being a lone Jew stranded on a far-off street, your exit blocked by a heavy-armed kike hater in a veteran's jacket.

They slowed down after a while and Stern put his arm around the girl's waist, as though he had been unable to stop and was using her to steady himself. Her neck was wet from the exercise, and the pungent dime-store fragrance of her hair brought him close to a delighted faint.

"Hey, you grabbin' my girl," said the blond boy, and, with a straight face, whipped a blue-veined, grenadelike fist into Stern's ulcer, stopping at the last possible instant and saying "Pow!" instead of landing the blow. Then he threw his head back and howled, saying, "You grab my girl, I got to give you one. Pow, pow, pow!"

"Suivez-moi to my petite habitat," said the girl, going up ahead of the group. "And a young girl shall lead them."

149

Not sure whether further waist encirclements were permissible, Stern walked beside her, and she said, "I used to work in a hardware store. You meet a princely selection of spooks there, it being near the main drag. One such spook came in one morning and said his friend wanted to spend the evening with me for $140. I asked him where yon friend was. He said he was across the street in a building watching the two of us with a telescope and would come down if I assented. I replied in the negative, of course. I'll entertain a man, to be sure, but not a telescoping type. You do agree there are many spooks in this land of ours." Stern, flattered that she had told him an anecdote, was not sure what to reply and decided he would tell her about his ulcer, testing her reaction.

"I've got something inside me. That's why I'm at the Home. I'm not sure how all this running around will affect me."

"The shits," she said. "I know them. The shits are a chore." She whirled around now and slid her fingers under the shirt of the tall, blond boy. "Does the darling midnight fool feel a cha-cha within him?" she asked. The blond boy took one hand off the wheelchair, tapped the underside of her breast, and said, "Flippety-flippety. Hey, Stern, you see that? Flippety-flippety."

The girl led them to the last house at the edge of a dead-end street; a sign saying "Tina's Beauty Salon" was in the center of the lawn alongside a thin and graceful tree. It had a white luminescent stripe across the bottom of its slender trunk, making it look like a thoroughbred horse's taped ankle.

"My queenly habitat," said the girl, and led them through the front door and down a long corridor with lined-up rows of hair-drying machines. She opened a door at the end of the corridor and guided them now into a small, sparely furnished room with a single bed and one

150

wall papered with Broadway show posters. The lamplight within was warm, making her features seem smoother and heightening the Tierney resemblance; Stern, weakened now by the bulge of her black sweater, the things she had been saying, and the show posters, wondered how it would be getting a divorce, being bled financially, and starting up anew with the Puerto Rican girl in this very room.

The girl flicked on a victrola, putting a finger to her lips, and said, "I'm just a tattered tenant here." She closed her eyes and swayed to the music as though it were a treatment; her body lagged a trifle behind the beat, in the slow-motion style of the feebleminded children she watched each day. Holding out her arms to the blond boy, she said, "Step inside this delightful sound." The blond boy came over, pinched her skirt, and said, "Check your oil." Then he pointed to the Greek boy, who sat staring out at the stars, rubbing his hands as though washing them in a sink. "Dance with George," said the blond boy. "Hey, George, dance with the broad." The Greek boy, his back to the others, a lawyer deciding a case, said, "I don't like dancing. I came out with you to do some jazzing."

The tall boy suddenly grabbed the Greek's wheelchair and pushed it out the door, saying, "I got an idea." Inside the beauty parlor room, he picked up a cigarette holder, put on a hairnet, and sat beneath a hair dryer. "Hey, look at me," he hollered back to Stern and the girl. "I'm an old broad."

The girl closed the door and said, "Boredom sets in swiftly." Still swaying to the music, she asked Stern, "What is your work?" Thrilled by her sudden interest and loving the way she had asked the question, Stern said, "Product labels. There's some writing to it, only not literary." Dancing with closed eyes and lagging behind the

151

beat, she said, "Someday I, too, shall write a volume. I shall include the sweetness and bile of my life." She stopped dancing now and said, "One of the spooks at the hardware store asked me to do some modeling. Bearded chap. Does figure work mean you work in the altogether, or does one get to keep a doodad on?"

"I don't get into that in my work," said Stern. "I don't like the sound of what you said, though. I have some friends who are legitimate photographers."

She changed the record to a fox-trot now and, taking off her skirt, said, "How would I look adorning magazines?"

Stern stopped breathing, and it suddenly came home to him that they were only a mile or so from the Grove Rest Home and that he was supposed to be undergoing treatment. He was certain that he would be caught, and he tried to imagine what untold horrors would await him if he were brought before the Home committee. At the very least they would throw him out, marking his records so that he would be banned from other rest homes when, at some later date, new illnesses came on. Then he imagined one gentile on the committee smiling thinly and saying, "No, no, let's let him stay," and then seeing to it that he was given a daily allotment of tarnished pills so that his stomach sprouted an entire forest of ulcers.

She put her hand on her hips in a terrible thirties pose and then took off her sweater, saying, "Oh yes, the bosom culture; I'd forgotten." Her breasts poured forward, capped by slanting, evil, Puerto Rican nipples, and Stern had a sudden feeling that his wife, at that very moment, sad-eyed and chattering with need, was hoisting her own sweater above her head in the rear seat of a limousine, that there was a strange sexual balance wheel at work, and that for every indiscretion of Stern's his wife would commit one too, at best only seconds later.

Like a discharged mortar shell, the tall, blond boy, a salivated look of rage on his face, charged into the room now and said, "Oh, you lookin' at my girl's nips, eh?" He shoved Stern against the wall and shot his fist at Stern's neck, stopping once again at the final instant and saying "Fwot" instead of landing the blow. Then he became convulsed with laughter, doubling up on the bed and howling, "I got you again." The boy stood up then and kissed the girl's nipples with loud, smacking sounds and said to the Greek, "Good set, eh?" Stern, feeling somehow that the girl's breasts were going to get hurt, walked over to her and said, "We were discussing something and she was demonstrating it." The tall boy said softly, "Oh, that's all right. I just like to diddle her boobs a little. George and me will take ten outside and kid around with those dryers." Then, with increasing kindness, he said, "You know the way you say things? Like what you just said? You were *discussing* something. That's nice. The way you have of saying all the thoughts in your head."

Stern noticed now for the first time that the boy's T-shirt had holes in it, and he felt very sorry for possibly having taken something away from him. What if his veins acted up and he had to spend six months in a room, unable to swing from trees and make believe he was going to hit Stern in the ulcer?

"We can all stay in here and play around," said Stern, but the blond boy walked out, saying, "That's all right, Mr. Stern, sir." To the boy in the wheelchair, Stern said, "You can stick around," but the Greek youth, rubbing his hands, said, "No, I don't feel like it tonight. You know, some nights you're just not in the mood for jazzing." He wheeled himself out of the room, closing the door behind him, and the girl put her arms around Stern's neck and said, "Sweet riddance. Now, my knighted author, will you be with me on the highest of all levels?"

Minutes previous, when she had taken off her clothes, Stern had planned merely to stare at her and fix her in his memory. Perhaps he would tap her behind and feel her breasts in the style of the other boys and then race back across the streets to the Grove Rest Home. It seemed to him that somehow if he did more, the Home would definitely hear of it, his treatment would be disrupted at an early stage, and he would be doomed to walk the streets forever with a permanent ulcer blooming between his ribs. And, of course, if he were to go further, within minutes his own wife, skirt gaping and great eyes confident, would sink back comfortably on the rear cushions of some strange convertible.

He waited for an outraged knock at the door, the clatter of Lennie's machine-shop legs, but nothing came and he fitted his hands over the girl's nylon-covered buttocks, thinking that he had never held a Puerto Rican behind before and that maybe it *was* a little different. She took his ear between her chipped white teeth, as though she were an animal pawing meat, and said, "Wondrous author of mine, explore forbidden avenues with deponent thine."

She guided him to the bed, did a dipping thing to make herself nude, and said, "Honest, do you think I'm sensitive?"

"Yes," said Stern, who loved the things she said.

She pulled him to her and said, "Then thrill my secret fibers." She put a contraceptive on him and said, "Now, honey, don't spoil it. Really, let's do a good one." It bothered Stern that she had the contraceptive on hand, but he liked the way she managed it, and the idea of her having one ready suddenly threw him into a frenzy. After a moment, she whispered, "We are as pages in a book of sonnets. Really give it to me." He said, "All right," and after a few seconds she rose and said, a little irritatedly,

"Oh, you thrilled me, all right. You really thrilled me."
She got into her clothes, and then the irritation passed,
and she perched on the bed beside him and said, "Such
loveliness I have never known." Her bare brown Puerto
Rican knees excited Stern and he wanted her again. He
had loved the things she whispered to him and the sting
of her teeth pulling on his flesh like meat. "Tell me of
your literary prowess," she said.

The door opened and the blond boy came in and said,
"We're tired of sitting around out there."

Stern looked out in the corridor and saw the Greek
boy's wheelchair against the window. He went outside
to him and found the boy crying. "My leg is gone," he
said. "I ain't got two fucking legs any more." Stern took
the boy's head against his waist and rubbed his neck,
trying to think of something to tell him. But there was
nothing. What could he say? That the leg would grow
back again? "Some people have things even worse than
legs in their stomachs," he said finally. He wheeled the
boy inside the room, where the girl sat perched on the
bed. The tall, blond boy picked up an extra-long broomstick handle and said, "Hey, George, let's give her a
ride." He quickly slid the broomstick between the girl's
legs, and the boy in the wheelchair, getting the idea,
dried his eyes, wheeled close, and caught the other end,
so that they had her straddling the stick as though she
were on a fence. They began to lift her up and down on
the broomstick, the two of them howling at the ceiling,
while the girl shouted, "Lemme off, you bastards." Stern
shouted, "You'll hurt her down there," but she looked so
awkward, he stopped loving her immediately. When she
cursed at them, Stern looked at her and said, "I can't
do anything."

"Hey, Mr. Stern, keep her up there," said the blond

boy, and Stern took the Greek boy's end and tossed her up and down a few times, saying, "I'm going to do this a little, too."

They finally let her down, and for an instant, straightening her skirt, she smoothed her hair and pretended nothing had happened. "Let me tell you further of my book," she said to Stern. But, after seeing her on the pole, the thought of her terrible Puerto Rican writing disgusted him and he said, "No literary stuff now."

She bent over then, holding her crotch, and said, "Ooh, you really hurt me down there, you cruddy bastards." Stern felt good that she had addressed all three of them, not excluding him, and it thrilled him to be flying out of her apartment with his new friends, all three howling and smacking each other with laughter at the pole episode. He wanted to be with them, not with her. He needed buddies, not a terrible Puerto Rican girl. He needed close friends to stand around a piano with and sing the Whiffenpoof song, arms around each other, perhaps before shipping out somewhere to war. If his dad got sick, he needed friends to stand in hospital corridors with him and grip his arm. He needed guys to stand back to back with him in bars and take on drunks. These were tattered, broken boys, one in a wheelchair, but they were buddies. They skidded across the lawn, wildly recalling the night's events.

The blond boy: "You see me kick that guy's ass? Pow, pow, pow!"

The Greek: "We almost ran that broomstick up the broad's kazoo, man."

Stern: "Did you see me hold that strong little guy at the bar?"

They split up at the main gate, each stealing back to his room separately. "Tomorrow night, maybe we do some real jazzing," said the boy in the wheelchair as they parted.

Exhilarated as he slipped past Lennie's darkened office, Stern, approaching his room, felt his stomach and was surprised to find the tapestry still prickling raw against it. Perhaps excitement is not good for it, he thought—even good excitement. But it did not really bother him, and it occurred to him for the first time that if necessary, by God, he would live with the damned thing. He opened his door now and saw the half man, bathrobe flown apart, toothache towel around his jaw, sitting on Stern's bed. The sleeping actor's foot stirred momentarily, tapping the edge of the bed in time to some forgotten vaudeville turn. Stern wheeled around in a panic, wanting to flee the room until the half man was out of there and his bed was scrubbed. He went out into the hall, but the half man chased and caught him, gripping Stern's wrist in a death vise. "Question," he radio-croaked in the dark hall.

"What?" asked Stern, his eyes closed so he would not see the half man, not daring to inhale lest he smell his halves.

"You Jewish?" the man asked, croaking so close his mouth worked against Stern's ear.

"Yes," said Stern, shutting his eyes until they hurt.

"Me, too," croaked the man, wheeling Stern around so that he had to face him. "I'm Jewish, too."

It did not thrill Stern to hear this. It was no great revelation, and it failed to touch him, just as the man's terrible violin playing had not moved him either. He said, "OK," and freed his wrist, but as he walked away a crumbling chill seemed to invade him, starting between his shoulder blades and pouring through all of him. He turned and kissed the man and hugged him and put his nose up

157

against the man's toothache towel, and then, perhaps using some of the courage he had amassed that evening, embraced the man's bad side, too.

He had counted on firm handshakes and hearty good-byes, exchanged phone numbers, pledges to continue friendships, and deep sincere looks in the eye, but on the morning of his departure he found that the people at Grove hung away from him. He was sitting on the porch with them, after leading the dumb march back from breakfast with Rooney in his arms, and he said to Rooney, "I'm all better and I'm going home today."

Rooney, who had been clinging to a pole and making waspish comments about the wealth of horse owners, turned to Stern and said, "You didn't say anything about that."

The old actor overheard Stern and said, "What did you come up for, if you were only staying such a little time? That's really country, boy, really country."

It was as though by getting healthy he had violated a rotted, fading charter of theirs and let them down. He had come into their sick club under false pretenses, enjoying the decayed rituals, and all the while his body wasn't ruined at all. He was secretly healthy, masquerading as a shattered man so that he could milk the benefits of their crumbling society. And now he felt bad about not being torn up as they were.

"I didn't know you weren't that sick," said Feldner in his bathrobe. "I had what you got, and I needed the warm of a stew in me every day for two years."

"I may have to come right back," said Stern, trying to make the man in the bathrobe feel better.

He went over to the charged-up blond boy, who was leaning on the young Greek's wheelchair, and said,

"Maybe you can take a run by my place when you get sprung."

But the camaraderie of the wild evening was gone. "You weren't even in here much," said the blond boy, and the Greek youth said, "Yeah, what'd you come up here—to fool around?"

Only Lennie was consistent that morning. He had taken Stern's baggage out of the room himself, and when Stern tried to help him, he said, "No infractions on last days. There are patients who rupture before check-out, and legal suits come about. Patients to the right as we take baggage downstairs." At the bottom of the steps, he loaded Stern's valises onto the baggage rack and walked intricately into his office. "Final pill," he said to Stern, getting one ready in a little cup. When the Negro handed him the pill cup, Stern stuck a folded-up five-dollar bill in the pocket of the intern's jacket. His mother had always stuck bills in the pockets of busboys and waiters and, after each insertion, had said, "I never missed that kind of money. You should see the respect I got for it." Lennie took the bill out of his jacket, examined it, and put it back in his pocket. He started to turn around, but then he changed his mind and asked Stern, "Anyone around?" Stern said everyone was out on the porch, and the Negro said, "Come on in here then," beckoning Stern into the forbidden office. "Have a seat," said Lennie, locking them both in. He sat down himself, releasing gears and switches, and then produced a loose-leaf notebook. He thumbed through it, stopped at a page, and said, "The old actor guy. Guy you roomin' with. He go around saying he got the weakness. He ain't coming out of here. They been trying to get him ready for another operation, but he too weak." He flipped the page and said, "Girl check in here two days ago," referring to a young and pretty

159

blond girl who had kept to herself. "She says she restin'. Well, she got something in her from intercoursin' with a man too big for her. Who else you want to know?"

"None of the others right now," said Stern, wanting to leave the room but afraid to offend the Negro.

"That's all right," said Lennie, turning to another page. "Rooney, the guy you carryin'. Bones softening up; nothing they can do on him. He be here for the duration." He flipped again. "Feldner, the Jew fella. He hit Casino. He gettin' out but ain't got no more'n a year." Without referring to the book, he said, "The half guy you see stalkin' around. He surprisin' everybody. He gawn be around when they all through."

The Negro ran through the other patients, while Stern made himself small in his chair and tried to block out all sound. After the last patient, Stern found himself putting another bill in the Negro's pocket, as though he hadn't realized what he was getting and saw now that he had underpaid.

A sweet and choirlike glow came over the Negro's face as he showed Stern out of the office and began to push the baggage cart. All the way to the administration building he blurted out secrets of the Home. "Nobody know it, but they get tranquilizer every day," he said. "Guy gonna die, we shift him to Room 12 so we can whip him out of there when he go and not shake up no one."

And after each batch of secrets, Stern compulsively stuffed another bill in the Negro's jacket, wanting him to stop and tell no others, yet paying him for each pair. On the front steps of the administration building, Stern saw his wife's car. The Negro, a little flustered, strained for a climactic one and finally said, "Staff get to eat better than the patients. We get better cuts of meat and all we want." Stern let Lennie get his bags on the car rack and stuffed a final five into his pocket.

"You didn't have to tell me any of those," Stern said, getting behind the wheel and taking his last look at the Grove Rest Home. But then, lest he hurt the Negro attendant's feelings, he said, "But thanks," and swept out of the driveway.

"I thought I'd always have it in there, but the parachute is gone," Stern told his wife as they drove home. "It feels as though I have a hot tablecloth around the front of me now, but it's better than the chute."

She sat beside him with one tanned leg folded beneath her, her great eyes glistening, wet with expectancy. She wore a cotton jumper, and when Stern leaned over to kiss her, he saw that her blouse was loose and he could make out the start of her nipples beneath her half bra. It got him nervous, and he said, "Why are you wearing your blouse like that? When you bend over, people can actually see the nipples. That isn't any damned good."

"It isn't?" she said, teasing him. "Oh well, don't worry; it's only when you get real close."

"None of that's funny," said Stern. "I just got out of the goddamned place for my stomach. Do you still go to that dance class?"

"Oh yes," she said, sitting against the door, her eyes huge. "That's what saved me when you were in there. First we dance like crazy and then we congregate at the overnight diner on Olivetti Street. That's the best part. You should hear one of the girls talk. Dirtier than anything you've ever heard. She's a scream. Then José spins me home, since he lives out our way."

"Is there any more of that tongue stuff?" Stern asked.

"Don't be silly," she said. "He kisses everybody. It's what they do."

She hung back against the door, her skirt above her browned knees, and Stern wondered whether she had

161

gone to bed with the instructor, getting into tangled, modern dance positions with him. How did he know she hadn't spent the entire five weeks of his sickness at endless, exhausting, intricately choreographed lovemaking, flying to the instructor seconds after she had deposited Stern at the Home? She seemed curled up, contented, shimmering with peace, as though someone had finally pressed the right buttons and relieved the dry, chattering hunger Stern had never been able to cope with. Perhaps she had gone to him in a desperate way, knowing that the instructor, however thin of bone and feminine of gesture, would never allow her to be insulted and would attack any offender with Latin fury. In any case, the secret was locked between her warm thighs. He would never know what had gone on, and he felt a drooping, weakened sensation and wondered why there couldn't be a chemical test, a litmus paper you could hold up to women to find out how many times they'd been to bed since last you saw them.

"We're having a recital and I've got to rehearse practically every night. It saved me while you were away. I'd have gone crazy."

"I don't know about any recitals," Stern said. "I've got to have everything easy on me. I don't want that thing coming back. I never want to go back to any rest homes. If I go back there, I'm really cooked."

At the Home, several days before Stern left, Rooney, hanging from an overhead porch beam, had told Stern of a merchant seaman who had gotten over an ulcer and who subsequently was incapable of being riled. "You could stick it into him from morning till midnight and he'd just give you a little smile and off he'd go like a contented cow." Now, as he drove home, Stern, who had spoken sharply to his wife and had felt the hot brocade tighten against the front of him, began suddenly to follow the

162

procedure of Rooney's man. He held the controls gently in his hands, tapping lightly on the foot pedals and scanning the road ahead easily, as if too vigorous a motion might topple his head from his shoulders. He began to do things in a slow and mincing way, as though he might be able to whisper and tiptoe through life, hushing his way past death itself. At the tollbooth, he smiled meltingly at the uniformed attendant, and when the man took his fifty cents, Stern said, "Thanks a lot."

"Why did you thank him?" his wife asked.

"Why not?" said Stern.

Later, when they approached the outskirts of Stern's town, they drove past small houses with neatly kept lawns and Stern nodded in a friendly way to the people who stood outside them. He knew they were all gentiles and he wondered what would happen in a pogrom. Which ones, if any, would hide him and his family from the authorities? Probably quite a few, he thought; ones that would surprise him. Probably the people with the most forbidding gentile faces. Ordinarily they'd never have anything to do with Stern, but if it came to a pogrom, with New England crustiness they'd spirit Stern and his family off to attics, saying to one another, "No one's going to tell us what to do with our Jews."

As they drove past the man's house, Stern held his breath and closed his eyes for a second, as though there were a chance it might not be there. He had been away five weeks, and perhaps part of his cure was that the man's house would be swept away or that it would disappear as though it had never been there, much like his vanished ulcer. But the house stood in the same place, and Stern, as he drove by, inclined his head gently toward it, as though he would face whatever horrors lay inside with softness and gentle ways, melting them with his niceness. As he neared his own house, he wondered fleetingly what he, the man down the street, would do in the event of a pogrom. Would he startle Stern by spiriting his despised Jewish neighbors away in his cellar, hating pogroms as even more un-American than Stern?

In his house, Stern sat down in the easy chair of his sparsely furnished living room and said to his wife, "Softly and easily. That's how it's going to have to be. No noise. No upsets."

His son came out with a bandage on his elbow and said, "What's it like to die?"

Stern said, "I'm not doing any dying for a while. But there'll be no rough playing any more. Everything with Daddy is soft and easy. Where did you get the cut? That's the kind of thing I don't want to get involved in, but where did you get it?"

"I found it on me in the morning," said the boy, beginning to suck a blanket.

Stern's wife, who had been boiling eggs for him in the kitchen, hollered in, "There's one last thing you're going to get a kick out of doing. The kind of thing you'll enjoy. I'll tell you about it later."

Stern started to eat the eggs, but they stuck in his throat and he said, "What's the thing? I don't want to get into anything two minutes after I'm back from a rest home."

"I wouldn't tell it to you, except it's the kind of thing you'll enjoy taking care of. Some kids came by on a bike, older than him, and one of them cut his elbow with a mirror and called him 'Matzoh.' I've been furious, but I saved it for you because I know it's the kind of thing you'll want to settle."

"He doesn't live around here, that bad boy," said Stern's son. "He's just visiting someone here. I wish you'd make the boy die."

164

"Daddies don't make small boys die," said Stern. The brocade that lay across the front of him began to heat up, and he pressed his fist deep into his stomach and held it there, on guard lest another ulcer begin to sprout forth and fill his ribs.

"Nobody seems to have heard what I've been saying," he said to his wife, but then he clasped his son's head and said, "You're right; it is the kind of thing I'd like to take care of." He took the boy to his car, squeezing his hand, and for a second it seemed that the child was really holding *his* hand, leading Stern and protecting him. He drove the car in a wide arc, as far as possible from the kike man's house, and the child said, "You're going too far. The bad boy won't be around here."

"You point him out to me," said Stern, the front of him on fire, crouched over as though to give the flames less area to ruin. They came to a cluster of seven boys who'd gotten off their bikes to rest, and Stern stopped the car, gripping his son's hand for courage. He went among them and said, "Someone said something to my son and cut him. They said a dirty thing to him, and it had better not happen again."

"Don't make them dead," his son said. "They're not the bad boys."

Stern grabbed the collar of one of them, twisted him close, and said, "I can really get sore, and when I do I can really start swinging. That better not happen again."

The boy looked at him evenly, without fear, and Stern released him. He must have been around twelve, and Stern wondered whether he would remember and two years later, at fourteen, with his body shaping into athletic hardness, come after Stern and pummel him to the ground.

Stern got back into the car with his son and, continuing

in the arc, he drove slowly through the streets and stopped alongside a small boy with glasses and large feet who was walking next to the curb, carrying books.

"Someone said something lousy to my son and cut him," Stern said from the car. "I don't like the particular kind of thing they said."

"I'm not a little boy," said the book carrier. "I'm seventeen and finishing high school. I'm small and everyone thinks I'm a kid."

"Don't make him dead, Daddy," said Stern's son. Stern felt very sorry for the small high-school student with his big feet, and yet he was thrilled to find someone in the neighborhood who read books and wasn't fierce. He wanted to invite him to his house and give him books, maybe take him to New York to see Broadway plays.

"Come over if you're near my place," said Stern, and drove off.

"I think the bad boy is visiting over there," said Stern's child, pointing in the direction of the house that darkened Stern's every waking moment. Nonetheless, he knitted his eyebrows, bared his teeth, and gunned the motor, as though, by going through the motions of outrage, he would somehow become outraged and the momentum would carry him right up to the man's front door before he had time to change his mind. He raced toward the man's house, and yet, when he reached it, the fraud of his facemaking became apparent to him and he continued on, realizing that he had never intended for a second confronting the man.

In his own home, Stern's wife asked, "Did you find him?" And Stern said, "I don't want to do any finding. Don't you realize I just came home from a Home a few hours ago?"

For one blissful second then, Stern's vision blurred and it seemed that he had gotten it all wrong, that he had not been away at all, and that he was to leave that very evening for a place where everything would be made better for him. But then he caught the edge of a chair, his eyes cleared, and he realized that he really had been away. The thought that he had come back to find his situation unchanged was maddening. It was as though he had been guaranteed that the treatment would heal his neighborhood as well as his ulcer—and that the guarantee had turned out to have secret clauses, rendering it worthless. The man was still there. The hospital had not had him removed. His wife had not somehow arranged to have him eliminated. His father had not gone down the street to thrust his scarred nose up in the man's face. No hand had reached down from the heavens and declared that the man had never existed. He was still right there in his house, not even seriously sick.

Stern went upstairs, and as he sat on the edge of his bed he felt a small spring inside him stretch and finally break, leaving his body in a great tremble. He lay back on the bed, as though mere contact with a bed could cure anything, but he could not quiet himself, and so he dialed Fabiola.

"A brand new thing has happened," Stern told him. "There's a tremble in me and I can't control it. The thing is, I've just come *back* from the damned rest home. Can you just come back from a place like that and have something like this happen?"

"Yes," said Fabiola. "You'd better avoid tension or you're going to wind up back there again. Remember that and call me if you get into more trouble."

Stern got on his knees now, as though in prayer, clutching fistfuls of sheet and trying to squeeze out the tremble. The bedroom windows were darkening with night when his wife appeared, flinging off her shorts, combing her hair, and saying, "I've got to go to rehearsals."

167

"Look," Stern said, "I'm going to ask you something, and I really have to. I've got a new thing and I have to have you here. I'm not talking about any ulcer but something really new and lousy."

"You mean you want me to give up the dancing? It's the only thing I have out here."

"You don't know what this new deal is," said Stern. As though to demonstrate, he began to take short, gasping breaths. It started as a plea for sympathy, but when he tried to stop he found he couldn't and he began to cry. "Let's get out of here. Oh, let's sell this house. We don't belong here. You'll have to handle all the details. Oh, I'm really in trouble now."

Part Four

It was a jangled, careening period that followed, and later he could remember it only as a black piece torn from his life rather than a number of days or weeks. He knew that it began trembling on the edge of a bed at midnight and he remembered how it ended, but he could pick out only single frenzied moments in between, as though it were all down on a giant mural he was examining in darkness with an unreliable flashlight. There was no good part of the day for him during this period, but it was the mornings that seemed the worst because there were always a giddy few minutes when it seemed he was going to be all right. But a dry, shriveling tremble would soon come over him, and it was then that he had to hold on to things, as though to keep himself on the ground. He held on to chairs and desks and he held on to himself, always keeping one fist buried deeply in his side, as though to nail himself down and join together the pieces of human spring that had snapped within him. Going to work was a stifled, desperate time, and there

171

was at least one ride when, sealed up in the train, holding the bottom of his seat with all his might, he thought he was not going to be able to make it and said to the man next to him, "I'm in a lot of trouble. You may have to grab me in a second." He remembered that the man, who smoked a pipe and wore his hat down low, had hardly looked surprised and said, "I'll keep an eye on you," and then gone back to his *Times*.

He was certain, on these rides to the city, that he would lose his breath and begin to bite things so that heavyset men, who'd been college athletes, would have to sit on him in mid-aisle, pressing his face to the floor, while conductors signaled on ahead to alert authorities. Each time the train pulled in, Stern would race gratefully to the street, sucking in hot blasts of summer air, stunned that he had made it.

In his office, on these mornings, a motor, powered by rocket fuels, ran at a dementedly high idle somewhere between his shoulder blades. He could not sit and he could not stand, and he remembered his narrow business room as a place to crouch and sweat and hope for time to pass. A film seemed to seal him off from the others around him. Unable to think, his mind an endless white lake, he touched papers and opened drawers and felt pencils, as though by physically going through remembered motions the work would get done. He did these things in short, frenzied bursts, holding on to a table with one hand; it seemed that someone was pulling him into the ground. At noon, his fist socked deep into his stomach, as though to seal it like a cork, he would run to a nearby park, where he would fling off his jacket, lie on his back, and stick his face in the sun, praying that he might sleep or disappear into the grass. Once he slept a long while in his office clothes, his face burning up in the heat. He awakened at a crazy, magical time of day, cool and grateful, the trembling stilled, and for a moment he thought it might be over. But then the motor turned over quietly and began to hum.

There was, too, during that period, a numb and choking fear of his boss, Belavista, that formed suddenly and oppressed Stern. He crouched within his office and gripped his desk and waited for the Brazilian to call. The man's confident morning steps in the hall sent Stern looking for a place to hide. The phone ring became a knife, and once, when it was late and Belavista summoned him, he flew first to the bathroom and locked the toilet stall. He could remember that later, in the front office, Belavista had stood for a long time without talking, his charred millionaire's face staring out of the skylight, while Stern died in his tracks. Turning finally, he had said, "How are things going in there?" And Stern, his tongue shriveling in his mouth, had said, "I just can't," and had run to put his face up to the park sun, grunting and squeezing his fists blood red, as though he could force and fight his way into a sleep.

His house, once he had screamed "Let's sell," became a dirty and infected place to Stern, and nights, returning home at a desperate clip, he could remember running lightly across the lawn, as though he did not want to make contact with the grass; lowering his head, so that he would not have to see the outside walls; and failing to touch the alien banister as he flew up to his bed, which was safe and clean and would go with him to the new place. He spent evenings on his bed, the cold sheets pacifying him, and he could remember a phone call after dark in which a man's voice had moaned out at him, "I saw your ad about the house. I don't want to know about anything but this: what kind of a neighborhood is it? I mean, is it mixed? Oh, I don't want it to be all my kind, but it's got to be half and half, a little of everything. I can't tell

173

you how important that part is." And Stern had moaned back, "Oh, I know; I really know," joining the man in tears.

There was a time when the house seemed the key to it all, an enemy that sucked oil and money and posted a kike-hating sentry down the street to await Stern's doom. But then Stern imagined himself on the twelfth story of a city apartment building, his house sold, sealed in now by new kike men, with different faces, occupying the three other apartments on his floor. He pictured himself high above the city at night, clawing at the windows. And during what must have been a weekend he told a solemn Swede who'd come to look the house over, "We have to stay here and have changed our mind."

The Swede, his head among a forest of basement pipes, hollered down, "Is it because I'm looking at the pipes?" And Stern said, "No, I'm too sick to move," and gave his wife the job of evicting the man.

Late at night, as he clutched his sheets in the darkness, ideas seemed to seize him by the throat, making him rock and cry and pray for sleep. The deep hot valleys of his wife's body frightened him now, and he could remember pulling her awake one night and saying, "You've got to get out of that dance thing. I know you don't go to bed with people, but the thought that you might is driving me crazy. I don't like to do this to you, but it'll just be for now, while I'm going through this thing."

"All right, I won't go to it any more."

"But that's not enough," he said. "What about every second I'm not with you? It would be easy for you to just pull up your skirt for someone. The second I leave the house. Or when you're just going alone somewhere. I'd never know."

"I'm not going to do anything," she said.

174

"I know, but you could. You could just flip up your skirt and open your legs and that would be it. It wouldn't take two minutes. And I don't want any man's thing in you. What would I do if that happened?"

"Well, then, what do you want me to do?"

"I don't know. But it's always going to be that way, all our lives." And he locked his hand around her wrist, as though only by holding her that way could he prevent her from flying out of the room in a desperate hunt for alien bodies.

He waited those nights for the trembling to stop, the engine to stop pumping. There had always been an end to bad things before—fevers dropped, homicidal dreams were chased by the dawn, and once, when he was a boy, his arm, heavy with a great infection, had suddenly fizzled and gone back to normal. But, now, it was as though he were an automobile with a broken horn, doomed to blare forever in a quiet residential neighborhood, all wiring experts having long been shipped out of the country. Sometimes, writhing and wet on the sheets at midnight, he would tell his wife, "I'm touching bottom," but it wasn't really true. He seemed to be holding on to a twig, halfway down a sheer, rain-slick mountain. How nice it would be to let go. But he had only $800, and it would be eaten up quickly if he were put in a sanatorium. He imagined himself in such a place at the end of three days, the $800 gone, in a terrible panic, unable even to lie back and be crazy with the other patients. And so he held on to the twig and he clutched at people, too, pulling at men's lapels and women's skirts on steaming city streets, telling them he was in bad trouble.

When it got so bad it seemed he'd have to smash himself against something to make the trembling stop, he would take some stranger's sleeve in the city and say, "I know this is going to sound crazy, but I'm pretty upset here and wish you would just talk to me a second." It amazed him that no one was perturbed by this. People seemed to welcome the chance to exchange wisdoms at midday with a strangulating young man. And Stern, no matter how banal their words, would attach great and profound significance to them, adopting each piece of advice as a slogan to live by. "I'm going to tell you something that's going to help you, fellow," an elderly gentleman said to him. "I was in trouble once, too, and I decided then and there never to give anyone more'n half a loaf. You remember that and you'll never go wrong again." And Stern said to him, "You know, that's right. I can see where, if you follow that, you'll always come out right." And he went off, determined to stop giving up entire loaves, convinced he had come up with the key to his trembling. A Negro ice-cream salesman told him, "You got to stop lookin' for things," and a retired jewelry executive, seized in a restaurant, advised him against "letting any person get hold of you." In both cases, Stern had said, "You know, you've really got it. I'm going to remember that."

He recalled being in many places and then running, choking, out of them. Once in a darkened, cavernlike restaurant, he ordered six lunchtime courses and thought to himself, "This is the end of it. I'm going to sit here like all the other men and eat, and when I leave this table it's all going to be over." But the service was slow, he lost his breath, and when the juice came, he gulped it down, threw out clumps of dollars, and flew from the pitlike restaurant, clawing for air. Another time, floundering across the hot city pavements, on an impulse he plunged into a physical culture studio and signed up for a six-year course. "I want to start right this minute," he said, and was shown to a locker. In shorts, he went into the gym, where the only person exercising was a great, bearlike man with oil-slick hair and huge, ballooning arms. He said to Stern, "Come here. Were you in the Army?"

"I was a flier," said Stern.

"I took a lot of crap from a drill sergeant in the Marines," said the man. "He'd stand out there, and the bullshit would come out of him in quart bottles, but do you know the only thing that saved me?"

"What's that?"

"His arms. They weren't even sixteens. I've got eighteens, myself. He'd stand there, and the shit would flow about how tough he was, but all you'd have to do is look at his arms and it didn't mean anything. How am I supposed to respect a man who doesn't have arms?"

"You can't," said Stern.

"Well, I'm going to do some arm work," the man said, and began to curl a great dumbbell into his lap. Stern watched his arms expand and said, "I can't seem to get started today." He dressed and then ran, gasping and unshowered, for the daylight.

Once, when the sound of Belavista's slippered footsteps down the hall sent him spinning into the streets, he ran into a telephone booth and called Fabiola.

"This thing isn't getting any better," he said. "It's like I swallowed an anthill. I'm jumping through my ass. You've got to send me to someone."

"Psychiatry's up in the air," said Fabiola. "There's the cost, too. Take a grain of pheno when you feel upset this way."

"I don't care about any expense. I don't think you know what's going on with me. It isn't the ulcer any more. I'd take a dozen of those compared to this new thing."

"All right, then," said Fabiola. "There's one good man. He's ten per session, and he *has* helped people."

"I really want to see him, then," said Stern.

The psychiatrist was a rail-thin man who talked with a lisp and whose office smelled musty and psychiatric. It bothered Stern that he had only one tiny diploma on the wall.

"Can it hurt me?" Stern asked.

"No," said the man. "Sometimes you dig down and come up with something very bad, but generally it helps."

"There's probably something lousy like that in me," said Stern. "How much is this going to cost?"

"Twenty a session."

Stern began to choke and said, "I heard ten. Oh God, I can't pay twenty." He gasped and sobbed and the man seemed to panic along with him.

"Maybe there's something about money," said the lisping psychiatrist. "Some people think it's dirty."

"No, no, it's the amount. Oh God, don't you just want to *help* people?" He got up, gasping, sucking in musty, psychiatric air, and the psychiatrist, gasping and white, too, said, "Maybe you think money has a smell. We could go into that."

"No, no," said Stern, "we're not going into anything. Imagine how you'd feel expecting ten and then hearing twenty." And with that he ran, crouching, through the door, with the panic-stricken psychiatrist hollering after him, "You've got a money neurosis."

One night, when for an hour or so there had been no gathering shriveling tremble inside him and it had seemed he might be done with it, he remembered being in a cramped and sultry theater with his wife, watching *Hedda Gabler*. He got through an act all right, but when Hedda tossed the writer's book manuscript into the furnace, he stood up in the stifling theater, shouted "Aye," and ran through the tiny exit, where he sat on the curb and waited for his wife.

Toward the end of it, he went everywhere with his arms folded tightly in front of him, as though he were naked in the snow. He bit down hard on things then, whatever was available—the drapes, a coffee cup, the corner of his desk—and yet there came over him, too, during this time, a kind of wild and gurgling courage he had never had before. Once, he ran with teeth clenched through a crowded train station, as though he were a quarterback going downfield, lashing out at people with his elbows, bulling along with his shoulders. One man said, "What do you think you're doing?" And Stern hollered back, "I didn't see you. You're insignificant-looking." When a cop stopped him for running through a stop sign, Stern heard himself saying, "Is this your idea of a crime? With what's going on in this country—rape and everything?" It was a perspiring, released kind of feeling he had when he was at his most desperate, and it gave him courage one day to seize a girl in his building who had seemed unapproachable. Tall and blond, with horn-rimmed glasses, she had a tight-skirted, whiplike body and spoke with a shrill, slightly hysterical British accent. Stern saw her in elevators for the most part, talking to a girl friend, a book on some declining civilization always pressed against her high, intellectual bosom. The word "problem" seemed to crop up in her every sentence.

"That's one of my problems."

"The man undoubtedly has a sexual problem."

Stern thought she was maddeningly intellectual and wanted to be with her in her small, book-lined apartment, kissing her hair as she discussed declining civilizations, spending long hours working out sick, tangled sexual problems.

One day outside the building, he took her arm and said, "This is crazy, but I don't know any other way to do it.

179

I've seen you a lot in the elevator, and I'm in pretty bad trouble now, and I wonder if you'd mind my just walking along awhile with you."

"I have to meet someone," she said.

"I'm in pretty bad shape," Stern said, holding on to her arm. "I've got a whole bunch of problems and I have to just tell them to someone."

"Yes," she said, freeing herself with a shrill little laugh. "But I don't like men's hands on me."

At the tail end of it, with courage forming along the bottom of him like vegetable shoots, it pleased him to make detailed and shocking phone calls to his mother and sister.

"I actually chew on drapes," he told his mother at midnight. "I pull at my skin and I won't have my job for long. I expect to go into an institution and not come out of it."

"I haven't had that in my life?" she said. "I haven't had much worse? I've had the same thing. You can't scare me."

"How would you like to see your son peeled off the fender of a speeding car? It's going to happen, you know."

And to his sister, long-distance, he said, "Oh, it's a breakdown, all right. Dying doesn't scare me in the least. It'll be in about a week or so. They're going to find me in a tub. I'll bet you're amazed that I can discuss it so calmly. Bet it really shakes you up to think it's happening to your own brother, who used to tell all those jokes."

He expected that if it ever did end, it would peter out, with a little less trembling and choking each day, but it surprised him by finishing up abruptly in a quite unexplainable way after a talk with a Polish woman who had come to clean his house.

Through it all, amazingly, he had never thought once of the kike man. Sliding down the mountain, he had been too busy casting about for things to clutch to think very much about who had pushed him. If the man had stopped him on the street, Stern, hunched over, fists planted in his waist to quiet the erupting, might have brushed on by and said, "I have no time to fool around."

On the night that it ended, his wife had gone to the movies, and Stern, a crawling, bone-deep shiver coming over him, had flicked off the television set and found the Polish woman on her knees in the broom closet. A small, pinched wrinkle of a woman, she seemed to have been made from a compound of flowered discount dresses, cleaning fluid, and lean Polish winters. She shook her head continually and muttered pieces of thoughts, finishing none of them. Stern talked to her for two hours and found her scattered, wise-sounding incantations soothing.

"You just can't," she said, rolling her head from side to side. "I mean you just don't go around. . . . You got to just . . . sooner or later. . . . I mean if a man don't. . . . This old world going to. . . . When a fully grown man. . . . Rolling up your sleeves is what . . ."

To which Stern said, "Oh God, how I appreciate this. I think I'm going to be able to get hold of myself now. I really do. Sometimes you just get together with a certain person and it really helps. I think I'm going to be all right. And, you know, as long as I live, I'm never going to forget this and the help you've given me. I really think I'm going to be able to stop it tonight."

"Sure," said the woman, rolling her head from side to side. "Of course. I mean you just . . . you got to. . . . There comes a time . . ."

And that night, when Stern's wife came home, he said, "I think I'm out of it." In bed, he relaxed his grip on the headboard, and then, just as swiftly as it had come over him, it more or less disappeared.

He told someone in his office, "I had the mildest nervous breakdown in town. I didn't miss a day of work. It was

181

pretty lousy, but all of a sudden you just come out of them." The two phrases "hanging on to desks" and "jumping through my tail" had great appeal to Stern, and he used them often to describe what had happened to him. He remembered a hairless boy with moonlike jowls who years back had worked for his company and had begun one afternoon to run into the water cooler. For two years, the boy had disappeared, taking mute and vacant vacations with his wife, renting clapboard houses and just sitting in them; Stern remembered seeing him on the street, looking white and clean as though someone had sponged him down. He looked up this boy's phone number now, called him, and said, "I just came out of one like yours. No water cooler, but I did a lot of hanging on to desks. I had to do it to keep from jumping through my tail. What are you doing with yourself these days?"

"Just sitting around," said the boy.

Stern had not thought of time or weather or clocks and dates and punctual changes of underwear, and he was certain that great clumps of dust had settled over his life; somehow, though, as he had choked and skidded and clutched at people's arms, he had managed to mail things, too, and pay dry cleaners. He expected to find his son making far-off, wistful comments about "new daddies" he would like to have, and yet the very first of the new evenings the boy tapped him on the shoulder and said, "Now can we play?"—as though he'd been waiting for Stern to finish tying a shoelace. "Yes," said Stern, falling to the floor. "I'm down here on the floor trapped and the only thing that can get me up is if someone touches a secret place on my ear three times and then taps me with a banana." The boy followed instructions delightedly, and Stern leaped up to shake his hand, saying, "Thank you for saving your daddy. I now owe you one hundred giraffe tails."

Stern looked at a calendar and saw that it had all worked out fine, ending on the first sharp and crackling day of October; now he would be able to draw winter down on himself and his family like a shade, huddling in his house and taking soups for strength. He had been too agonized and out of breath to think about his stomach, and it amazed him that it was not leaping with a fresh crop of ulcers; it seemed to be doing all right, the glue holding firm on a cracked china cup. Maybe that was the trick. Go into a tumbling, frenzied period and your stomach simply wouldn't have time to concentrate on ulcers. The idea was to set up small, diversionary troubles in other parts of your body, way out on your fingers or inside your head. But what if now, with things quieter, a new batch got under way?

He wanted to take the previous weeks in his hands, crush them down to snowball size, and examine them close to a light bulb so that he would understand them if they happened again. It seemed a time to talk, finally, about dramatic central things, death and wills and horrible, long-buried family crises from which lessons could be drawn. First he called his insurance man, who said, "Before we go any further, remember, you can't dictate from the grave." And then he called his mother, telling her, "I really want to have a talk now. You don't know what hell I've been through."

"I know what you've been through and, believe me, I could tell you a few things. I could tell you things that would stand your hair on end."

"All right, tell me them then."

"Don't worry," she said. "I could tell you plenty. I could fill up books if you really wanted to listen."

"Meanwhile you haven't said anything."

"Someday, when you're ready, I'll say plenty. Then you

won't wonder why I take an occasional drink. And then, years later, you'll tell people, 'I had some mother.'"

He met his father for dinner in the city, and much of the conversation had to do with the machinery of the meeting. "How long have you been waiting?" his father said, outside the restaurant. "I thought I'd take a cross-town bus, get myself a transfer, and then walk the extra two blocks over to Sixth. If I'd known you were going to be early, I'd have come all the way up by subway and the hell with the walking. How'd you get up here?"

"I just got here," said Stern. "I want to talk over some things with you."

Inside the restaurant, Stern's father kept grabbing the elbows of waiters and customers, turning to Stern, and saying, "You know how long I know this guy?" Stern would guess, and his father would say, "I know this guy for seventeen years" or "We go all the way back to 1933," bobbing his head up and down, as though to testify he was telling the truth, however astonishing the statement may have seemed.

During dinner, Stern said, "I went through a cruddy period. I don't know what in the hell hit me."

"I heard," said his father. "You know how I feel about you, though, don't you?"

After a while, his father said, "How do you plan on getting back? I think, in your situation, your best bet is to walk over west and catch a bus going downtown. Lets you off slightly north of the station. You can duck down and walk the rest of the way underground or, if you like, you can grab a cab. I haven't figured out how I'm going home myself. . . ."

Often now, for the first time since it had happened, Stern was able to see the bitter episode in his recent life for what it was: an ignorant remark, a harmless shove, no one really hurt, much time elapsed, so what. Yet, other times, the thought of it became unbearable and he would try to shore up his mind against it. Then it was as though his head were a leaky basement which Stern patrolled from the inside, running over with plaster each time a picture of the man down the street threatened to slide in through a crack. One night, the basement leaked in so many places he could not get to them all.

He had come back after a short visit to what his son called "the slippery houses," a group of high, slanted, darkening hill peaks, all clumped together in a tilted village with cottages stuck on the sides like canapés. "We ought to get out of our house and see what it's like around us," Stern had said to his wife and son, but they had always wound up taking a silent, peculiar drive to this one place. Their car could barely make it up the hills of the careening village, and Stern wondered what kind of people lived in such a strange, slanted place. It seemed you would have to be lowered down to your neighbor's house, if you wanted to do any visiting, and then hoisted back. He wondered what kind of tilted lives the people inside the houses led, what kind of wobbly activities they were up to, and whether they would come clinging and suction-footed to the door if he rang the bell. In all the visits, they saw only one person who lived in the village, a pointy-headed boy of the sort who was always being sent to town with bread and cheese and several farthings and then set upon immediately by rascals.

Back home after the drive that night, Stern's son asked him if dinosaurs were good, and when Stern said, "There were all kinds," the boy asked, "How about pirates? Were any of them daddies?"

"Some pirates were daddies," said Stern.

During his troubled, spinning weeks, Stern had often brushed by the child, saying, "No elephants, no whale questions," and gone to hold on to something or to lie somewhere in a sweat. Now, as though to make up for his brusqueness, he held talks with the boy on an almost formal schedule.

"I can remember being inside Mommy," said the child, taking off Stern's shoe. "I knew about the Three Stooges in there. Now I'm taking your foot's temperature. It's quarter past five."

During dinner, the boy said, "Were you ever a magician before you became my father?"

"Right before," said Stern.

"Could you tear a Kleenex into a thousand pieces and then turn it back into a whole Kleenex again?"

"I could do that one."

"Do you learn about the inside of soda at college?"

"I don't know," said Stern. "I don't know that. No soda now. No pirates. I'm just going to sit here." He was eating an apricot dessert then, and he began to breathe so hard he thought something would fly out of his chest. "I've got to go out and get some air," he told his wife.

"Is it all right for daddies to go out in the dark?" asked the boy, and Stern said, "If they're very careful."

Outside, walking on leaves, Stern could not catch his breath and wondered if he should call a cab. He saw himself walking all the way to the man's house only to collapse, wordless and exhausted, on the doorstep, having to be put outside near the garbage for someone to see and take home. He thought it was unfair for him to be depleting his strength in a long, cold walk while the man sat in a tasteless but comfortable armchair, his forearms bulging after a day at the lathe.

When he had gone a few hundred feet, he thought of turning around and telling his wife where he was headed or at least leaving a note on the porch so that someone would know his whereabouts in case he wound up cracked

186

and bleeding, the life seeping out of him, yet completely out of public view. He imagined people saying of him later, "The funny part is they could have saved him if only they'd been able to find him in time." He thought that perhaps he would find a man on the way, have him stand by, and, as soon as Stern's head hit a pipe or something, speed off to get an intern. The cold snapped about him now and seemed to have made everything a little harder. There would be no soft earth to fall into, and any contact at all with the ground would mean great, tearing skin scrapes.

When he was halfway to the man's house, it crossed his mind for the briefest instant that the fluids drained from the bodies of unconscious people, and as a precaution against this embarrassment he stopped to urinate in some leaves. He was worried about being completely unable to talk when he got to the man's house, knocking at the door and then standing there, cold and choking, while the man inspected him. He had heard that if you did some physical exercise, tension would flow out of you, and once, before an important job interview, he had run briskly around the block. "Have you been running?" the interviewer asked, and Stern said, "I didn't want to be late." The run had checked the tension, but Stern had gasped incoherently through the interview and come off poorly.

Now he began to jog a little through the leaves; when he came to the man's house, he took a long time before actually setting foot on his property, a move which somehow would have made the visit irrevocable. He thought of just putting his heel inside the fence, crushing the grass down a bit, and then going back home and getting his mind so elastic and sophisticated he'd be able to see that crushing a little grass was defiance, too. It didn't have to be face-punching. But when he put one foot inside, he took another step, too, and then another, a man going into a cold pool, and then walked the rest of the way to the door at a brisk, routine pace, as though by walking routinely he could turn this into a routine call.

There was a simple stone walk through some short grass and a step leading up to a brown oaken door. He had expected the house to have some memorable characteristics, symphonic music to play when he actually set foot inside the fence. He knocked on the door and suddenly shook with hope that the wife would answer and say she was sorry but the man was attending a meeting of the Guardian Sons. It was an election meeting to select officers who would be even more pinched and thin-lipped than the old crew. He would say to the woman, "Your husband said something to my wife and I want to say I know about it and he's not getting away with it. You tell him that." Then he would be able to go back home, his mission accomplished. After all, he had tried. It wasn't his fault the man was not in.

The man opened the door and Stern blinked to see him better, startled that although he stood only two feet away, he still could not really make out his face. It was as though he were looking at the man through an old pair of Japanese binoculars he had once bought. They were expensive, but Stern had never quite gotten them adjusted right and always saw things better with his eyes. He could see that the man was shoeless, however; wore blue jeans and a T-shirt; and kept his head cocked a little in the incredulous style Stern remembered so clearly. The beer had taken some effect; he seemed a little heavier than Stern recalled. His arms were about the same, perhaps a little thicker in the foresection than they had seemed to be from the car.

"Are you the man who said kike to my wife?" asked Stern, happy he had only short sentences to get out.

"I think I remember that."

"About a year and a half ago?"

"That's right."

"You shouldn't say that, and we're going to fight."

"All right. Let me get my slippers on."

Stern had not expected any delays, and when the man closed the screen door he thought of how little insurance he had and wondered if he could call out, "Excuse me just a minute," and run back to take out another policy, then return. He wanted so bad to live he would have settled right on the spot for being a bedpan patient all his life. If only there were someone with whom he could enter into such a bargain. The man came back and said, "Come on around back here," walking toward the rear of the house, and Stern did not follow. He remembered that he had not brought along an observer to run for an intern and wondered if he could hail one now, not to stop the fight, but just to stand by and watch it and know that it was going on. He thought that maybe the man's wife was watching through the shades and, if Stern's head were opened, *she* would call for help, waiting first until he was almost through. He wanted to stop what was happening, take the man aside, and say, "Look, the important thing was for me to come down here. Now that I'm here, there doesn't have to be any fight. I didn't think I could make it, but here I am, and why don't I just go back now?" But, instead, he followed the man to the backyard and said, "I don't know how to begin these." The man paused a moment and then hit Stern on the ear, a great freezing kiss covering the entire side of his face. The lobe seemed to slide around a little before settling in one place, and Stern was so thrilled at still being alive he jumped a little off the ground. But then his joy was erased by a warm shudder of sympathy for the man, who had been unable to knock him unconscious with the blow. It was as though all those years at lathes, building arm power, had gone to

189

waste. More because it seemed to be expected of him than because he felt anger, Stern tried to throw a punch in the smoothly coordinated style of a Virgin Islands middleweight he had watched on TV, but it was as though a belt had been dropped over him, constricting his arms, and the blow came out girlish and ineffectual. Lowering his voice several octaves, as if it were he who had delivered the ear kiss, he said, "Don't talk that way to someone's wife and push her," and only after he had said it did he realize he had fallen into an imitation of an old deep-voiced high-school gym teacher who used to say, "Now, boys, eat soup and b'daders if you want your roughage."

"Shit I won't," said the man, and Stern said, "You better not," still blinking to see the man's face. He saw his socks, though, faded blue anklets with little green clocks on them. They were cut low, almost disappearing into his slippers, and reminded Stern of those worn by an exchange student from Latvia at college who had brought along an entire bundle of similar ones. Now Stern felt deeply sorry for the man's powerful feet, which were always to be encased in terrible refugee anklets, and for a second he wanted to embrace them.

His ear began to leak now, and he walked off the man's lawn, not sure at all how he had done. The hot flush of exhilaration that had come with the punch stayed with him awhile, and yet when he had gone halfway back to his house the cold flew into his shirt and rode his back and he began to shake with fear of the man all over again. Inside his house, his wife was sponging the dinner table and said, "What happened to your ear? It's hanging all off."

"I had a fight with that guy from a year and a half ago. The one who said the thing to you. I can't understand it. I was all right for a while, but now I'm afraid of him all over again."

"That's some ear you've got," she said.

"Ears never worried me," he said. "I don't understand why I still have to be afraid of the bastard. Come on upstairs." They walked to the steps and his wife said, "You go first. I don't like to go upstairs in front of people." And Stern went on ahead, annoyed at being denied several seconds of behind glimpses.

Upstairs, in his son's room, he looked at the six or seven children's books on the floor. Pages were torn out of them, and Stern wondered how the child was ever to become brilliant on so ratty-looking a library. Once, in some kind of sheltering, warmth-giving act he really couldn't explain, Stern had bought children's rugs and hung them all over the walls. The boy had said, "Rugs on the wall?" And Stern had answered, "Of course, and we put pictures on the floors, too. We eat breakfast at night and get up in the morning for a bite of supper. This is a crazy house."

Now Stern walked around the room, touching the rugs to make sure they wouldn't fall on his son's face. Then he said, "I feel like doing some hugging," and knelt beside the sleeping boy, inhaling his pajamas and putting his arm over him. His wife was at the door and Stern said, "I want you in here, too." She came over, and it occurred to him that he would like to try something a little theatrical, just kneel there quietly with his arms protectively draped around his wife and child. He tried it and wound up holding them a fraction longer than he'd intended.